Hiram Orcutt

Reminiscences of School Life

An autobiography

Hiram Orcutt

Reminiscences of School Life
An autobiography

ISBN/EAN: 9783337027957

Printed in Europe, USA, Canada, Australia, Japan

Cover: Foto ©Raphael Reischuk / pixelio.de

More available books at **www.hansebooks.com**

Reminiscences of School Life

An Autobiography

By HIRAM ORCUTT, LL.D.

With an Introduction by General John Eaton

Ex-U. S. Commissioner of Education

Cambridge

PRINTED BY THE UNIVERSITY PRESS

1898

TO

The Five Thousand Pupils

WHO, DURING FORTY YEARS, SHARED WITH HIM AS
THEIR TEACHER THE PLEASURES AND
TRIALS OF SCHOOL LIFE,

THIS LITTLE VOLUME

IS AFFECTIONATELY INSCRIBED BY THE AUTHOR.

Preface

THIS book is the record of a long
and eventful school-life experience.
It treats not of theories, but of facts. It is
an autobiography, and, as its title indicates,
records not only the author's experience
as a practical teacher in the public school,
academy, and seminary, but also as a pupil
and student, all covering a period of three-
quarters of a century. The leading purpose
of the work is to furnish teachers, school
officers, parents, and citizens who have an
interest in our private and public schools,
object lessons illustrating the principles
and methods which the author advocated
in public address, and in his earlier books,
and adopted in his school management and
discipline.

The reminiscences include the incidents
and anecdotes which interested him all

along the way in his boyhood and in active life. They trace the trials and struggles of the poor young man in his efforts to gain a liberal education. They take note of the changes which the process of evolution has wrought in the educational history of the country, comparing the old institutions with the new. The author comments upon the condition of these institutions and upon their relations to each other, and illustrates his method of dealing with patrons and in conducting the different schools over which he presided. He discusses the elements of success in school life, and estimates the profit and loss of the poor boy's struggles to secure an education. His experience as preceptor of large academies and seminaries was unique. No one of the four institutions under his charge had any other means of support than the receipts derived from a low rate of tuition, and he was never employed on a salary during the thirty-eight years of his academic life. These institutions gave opportunity for experience in managing both mixed and separate schools, and enabled him to test the merits of each system. Hence, upon this subject and upon the higher education of women he has expressed positive convictions.

In connection with his treatment of school life as student and teacher he has discussed the elements of success, and given hints and suggestions for the guidance of the inexperienced. In the chapter on other educational work he has dwelt upon the teacher's relations and obligations to the community in which he lives, and the cause in which all have a common interest. He speaks of the importance of journalism, educational and professional books, and teachers' bureaus as aids to educational workers, and of the part he has acted in these relations.

It has been the endeavor of the author throughout these pages to emphasize the fact that the real end of all education is to produce morally trained *men* and *women*, rather than, except in special cases, *scholars*. Unless this point is kept in mind by the

Preface

teacher throughout his school-life experience, the professional element of his chosen vocation fails utterly of its chief end, and the pedagogue places himself in the same class as the mechanic, producing things instead of creating characters.

The author trusts that this humble effort to contribute to the progress of the great cause vital to the perpetuity of our free institutions and the welfare of our race, to which he early consecrated his life, may serve to interest and encourage others who may have taken up this important work.

HIRAM ORCUTT.

April 8, 1898.

Contents

Introduction

INVITED to write here a word of introduction, my belief in the large obligations of the child to the parent, and of the pupil to the teacher, prompts me to respond with alacrity, — an alacrity all the greater because I am not expected to assent in all things to what the author has put down, any more than I was required when his pupil to accept blindly his dicta as my master; for he always expected differences of opinion, and only demanded robust thinking responsive to the leadings of truth. It was my good fortune to come under his influence when I began to have aspiration for opportunities to study. The way was dark and the obstacles seemed insurmountable : he had some two hundred and fifty young men and women under his instruction. No endowment either

Introduction

INVITED to write here a word of
introduction, my belief in the large
obligations of the child to the parent, and
of the pupil to the teacher, prompts me to
respond with alacrity, — an alacrity all the
greater because I am not expected to assent in all things to what the author has
put down, any more than I was required
when his pupil to accept blindly his dicta
as my master; for he always expected
differences of opinion, and only demanded
robust thinking responsive to the leadings
of truth. It was my good fortune to come
under his influence when I began to have
aspiration for opportunities to study. The
way was dark and the obstacles seemed insurmountable : he had some two hundred
and fifty young men and women under
his instruction. No endowment either

I

paid teachers or aided students. His management was the sole resource. When considering it I have always marvelled; but he had the time and thought for me as he had for each of all the others. My way opened; I was inspired with new hope through him, and further encouraged by his students with whom I associated and on whom his influence took effect. New purposes possessed me; obstacles were transformed into aids; another life opened before me. Can I ever repay him?

He has seen fit at the age of fourscore and more years to set down so much of his experiences and of the opinions which he has formed on important subjects. We are greatly lacking in the knowledge of the personal experiences of teachers. As our views of history, in general, are greatly helped by the biography of those who were its actors, so our best ideas of the special history of education must be gained by the study of the lives of educators. The upward steps in its philosophy will be best disclosed through their experi-

Introduction

ences and views. The literature of education is multiplying with rapidity, and
the profession of teaching needs some
one to do for it what Dr. Sprague did
for the ministry. Nay, all other pursuits would be benefited by such a service;
for all, whatever careers they pursue in
life, come under the forming hand of the
teacher.

A legend has it that " When the temple
at Jerusalem was completed, King Solomon
gave a feast to the artificers employed in
its construction. On unveiling the throne,
it was found that a smith had usurped the
seat of honor on the right of the king's
place, not yet awarded; whereupon the
people murmured and the guard rushed
to cut him down. 'Hold, let him speak,'
commanded Solomon. 'Thou hast, O
King, invited all craftsmen but me, yet
how could these builders have raised the
temple without the tools I fashioned?'
'True,' decreed Solomon, 'the seat is his
by right.'" Art has seized and preserved
the idea representing the blacksmith in
the seat of honor on the right of the

3

throne. Teaching is no longer classed as menial service. The advance in man's progress is coming to give the seat of honor to the teacher who shapes the characters for all worthy pursuits, — who fits all instruments for the upbuilding of the temple of human affairs; thus teaching is coming into its true relation to all other pursuits. This book leaves no doubt that Dr. Orcutt has, in his day, greatly aided in improving the work of the teacher and in securing his recognition by his fellows. Generally, men divide themselves into two classes, — those who do and those who say. He has both acted and spoken; as teacher he has taught the pupil in his daily class-work; he has made a career; he has built up institutions; he has also spoken from the platform and the pulpit; written much for the press; and as the author of books he has been widely read, thus greatly extending his influence. His inheritance did not do this; he started with none of the aids of wealth, station, or money of which so much is made and upon which so many depend. His greatest inheritance was a

nature strong and healthy, both mentally
and physically. He was born on a farm,
and his childhood and youth were occupied
in tilling the soil, in the rock-ribbed town
of Acworth, New Hampshire; " All was
industry from early morn till dewy eve;"
few books were accessible, and there were
limited opportunities for cultivating the
mind; but he was in the midst of the cus-
toms, scenes, and dutiful ideas common in
a New England community before those
transformations of its character came which
have followed the changes incident to the
introduction of the inventions of the last
three-quarters of our century. He became
possessed of the idea of his own improvement and of service to his fellows and to his
Maker. It grew with his growth, and has
extended through his life, binding its acts
together, — a purpose which, taking hold on
the throne of God, has carried him through
his trials and assured his triumphs. He
could not have had any degree of advanced
education save as he paid for it out of his
own earnings; his course had to be a division
between existing and improving himself;

thus only could he fit for college and avail himself of collegiate training; he might lament that he could give no more time to study; it was a constant struggle to answer the question — How little time can I devote to existence and how much to improving myself? This story gives the result. He learned to discriminate between the essential and the non-essential, to seize the substance and let the shadow take care of itself, to economize time and power, and to make the best of all things. His career has been onward, and illustrates the possibilities of American opportunity, of New England opportunity. His great labors as teacher were, like those of his student life, unaided by the usual funds. He made his schools; his efficiency was their endowment; his beneficence and not the gifts of others furnished the money to supplement the means of the hundreds of students, men and women, whom he aided.

I would neither ignore nor disparage the conditions of education which money may furnish in the libraries, buildings, and endowments and other aids. It has been my pleasure to improve every opportunity to urge these services upon those who possess wealth. Indeed, wealth must share in giving the means, and thus assuring for the young of all conditions the best culture of all grades from the lowest to the highest, if its possessors would enjoy the prosperity and security possible only in an advanced order of society. But with this urgency I would have the fact understood that there is something in education which money cannot furnish. I would not have forgotten the truth set forth in Garfield's argument in the case of " Brains *vs*. Brick and Mortar." I wish that all might understand what he meant when he was ready to put all appliances aside and declared his preference for a plank or a plain table and Mark Hopkins as a teacher at one end if he could be the pupil at the other. In all treatment of the conditions of learning justice demands discrimination. When wisely urging permanency, strength, great equipment and endowment, we must not forget what temporary academies and colleges under masters of teaching have accomplished; nor what our aspiring Franklins and Lincolns have done without coming within the sacred influence of a college curriculum; nor must we ignore the influence of the small college, as we have good reasons to remember — and especially from the fact that it was not a great institution at the time but a small college — Dartmouth in its infancy, that trained Webster, the mightiest thinker of his period, whose defence of the college he loved led to a judicial decree which under our National Constitution has been the rock of safety for all chartered institutions whether great or small. The students' aspiration and the teacher's power to awake to better thought and life are the essentials. To inspire the pupil to his best effort was pre-eminently the power of our author. In this light we should contemplate his life. A thought enters his boyish mind of improving himself; he struggles amid hardships without the aids upon which most predicate success; he works with his hands and toils as a teacher, to earn the money

to pay the expenses of his course of study.
He learns self-restraint, and that he can
live on what others would waste; he suc-
ceeds where others have failed; he revives
old and opens new seats of learning; he
fills them with eager students, meeting all
demands for expenses without endowment and without the usual bids for exclusively wealthy patronage; indeed, his
tuitions were so moderate that all, even the
plain people, could pay them. His great
cares are not made excuses for neglect of
other duties. As head of the family he is
the devoted husband and father, greatly
revered and tenderly loved; as citizen he
is alert and ready to administer the responsibilities demanded of him; chosen as leg-
islator by his townsmen, as a statesman he
is ready for the higher issues and seizes the
opportunity to found a normal school for
the State; in business affairs he is at once
ready for large demands and attentive to
details; in the Church he is reverent and
active in its duties; and amid all he finds
time to use his pen. To get some measure
of his influence, mark the procession which

he leads! At the front are the hundreds trained by him in the district school; next come the thousands in the academies under his management; while these are followed by those who have been otherwise directly influenced by his touch or his pen; and following these are the untold numbers who have felt the influences set in motion by him as they have multiplied themselves in this and other lands through those inspired to their worthy work under God by him. How many rise up to call him blessed! Have they any doubt that his is a life worth living? They know how he has taught patriotism, piety, and duty in the smallest and largest affairs. They know how he has in his day added to the security of the family, the Church, and the State those foundations divinely laid, upon which all things depend that are desirable in human affairs.

I am one of those who rejoice in his triumphs; one of those gratified to seek the general acknowledgment of the fitness of the laurels which crown his brow as he passes down his declining years; and I pray that this story may extend his usefulness for good, and that there may be an increase of Hiram Orcutts for coming generations.

JOHN EATON.

WASHINGTON, D. C.

Reminiscences of School Life

THE OLD DISTRICT SCHOOL

MORE than three-quarters of a century has elapsed since the writer entered his first school, as a pupil; yet everything associated with that school is as fresh in memory as the occurrences of yesterday. The old schoolhouse, the teachers, the schoolmates, and the incidents of that period of school life are photographed in distinct outlines on memory's page.

That antiquated schoolhouse stood on "Clark Hill," in the town of Acworth, New Hampshire. It was built upon a rock, and surrounded by boulders which the icebergs of another age had scattered there. The only shade-trees that adorned the playground were those which the sturdy woodman had spared in clearing the forest. The building was rude and simple in its construction. It had three small windows on as many sides, each of which had a heavy board shutter to keep out the light during vacations, and to conceal the bats in term-time. They served both purposes well. The bats, however, were easily captured by the roguish boys, and sometimes made trouble for the master. The inside arrangements of this school-house were unique. On one side was a large open fireplace, which with its entrance door occupied the whole space. In this great heater, in the cold winter, not less than half a cord of green wood was consumed each day, roasting half the school and leaving the other half nearly frozen during the process. The seats and benches were made of half-planed hemlock or spruce boards, and were arranged on three sides of the house, in amphitheatre style. The back seats were designed for the older boys and girls, and the front seats for the

little ones sent to school to relieve the
mothers of their care at home. These
seats were so wide that the child's back
could not be supported, and so high that
his feet could not touch the floor. A
more complete rack of torture and machine
for making cripples could hardly be in-
vented. Yet these children were kept
upon these hard benches all day long,
relieved only by short recesses, with nothing to do but to play, if they dared.

In one respect that old schoolhouse was
a model of its kind, far superior to many
of more modern construction; it was well
ventilated. Its huge open fireplace, spacious chimney, loose windows, and half-
nailed covering boards invited the passing
breeze and gave free circulation to the pure
mountain air. No pupil ever contracted
consumption from breathing impure atmosphere in that temple of knowledge. This
cannot be said of many elegantly constructed and steam-heated schoolrooms of
modern times, if special attention has not
been given to scientific ventilation.

Another advantage enjoyed by the pupils

of that ancient school on "Clark Hill" was the exercise necessary in going and coming. Added to the rough and tumble of schoolboy sports, and battles of snow-balling, some pupils lived two miles away, making four miles' walk each day over rough or snow-drifted roads. The dinner-basket was a necessity; and even the rats and mice which had gained residence in the old schoolhouse were dependent for their living upon the crumbs that fell from the benches, when they failed to gain access to the full basket. Still we were not much annoyed by them. No one thought to inquire as to the origin of the different animal races, or whether the bats which lived under the blinds and the quadrupeds which scampered behind the ceiling were created as such or were born of evolution. This old school building was the scene of busy life during ten or twelve weeks both summer and winter. The remaining part of the year, it was deserted and desolate.

The teachers employed in this district — a young man in the winter and a young

woman in the summer — deserve a passing
notice. They "kept school" one term
each, but were seldom re-elected. As a
matter of fact these teachers were incom-
petent. They had enjoyed no opportunity
for culture and professional training. It
was not their fault. There were no training schools in those days, no examinations,
no opportunities nor inducements to gain
the necessary preparation for their important work. The parents of the pupils had
inherited the *idea* of education for their
children, but knew little or nothing of
its nature or importance. Economy was
the main concern with them. Hence the
scanty outfit for school purposes, and
the cheap teachers. The question as to the
candidate's qualifications for the teacher's
office was seldom raised, but rather how
small a compensation would be accepted for
the service required. In fact, the school
was "struck off" to the lowest bidder.
That was not economy, but a ruinous waste.

In that school, and in almost all other
country schools of that day, there was no
systematic instruction, no class-drill, little

mental discipline, and absolutely no practical training for even the common duties of life. Incorrect instruction led to the formation of bad habits of thought and study. These had to be corrected before any real progress could be made. The writer received as much real benefit from study at home, and more knowledge of English composition from correspondence with a playmate in vacations, than from all the instruction he ever had in the district school. This correspondence, or written discussion with a companion, here alluded to, was a novelty of its kind. The old farmhouses where our boyhood days were spent were a mile distant from each other. We were frequently together, but differed in our opinions on some of the current topics of the day. It was proposed that we engage in a written discussion. We agreed upon the subject and the method of the contest. On the roadside half-way between our houses, there was a large shelving rock under which we agreed to locate our post-office, and deposit our letters in turn. Though we might not see each other for weeks, the discussion went on to the finish. Thus the benefit of independent thinking and reasoning and the power of expression were gained. Could we have had a competent critic of our forensic effort, this would have been a model exercise worthy of modern times.

While yet at home on my father's farm (which lay one half in the town of Acworth and the other half in the town of Unity), I made my first effort to write for the press. It was called out under the following circumstances. One Fourth of July, a large number of boys and young men living in Acworth and Unity assembled in the field near the house, on the Acworth side, for a wrestling match between the two towns. The struggle was at "arm's length," each victor meeting the man selected by a committee on the other side. I threw my man and was thrown in turn. The contest lasted all day; and at night both parties claimed the victory, and I was appointed by the Acworth boys to write a report of the contest in vindication of our claim, for publication in a local newspaper.

As I remember, I claimed that we had shown superior strength and skill in the match, and had in reserve a still greater force ready to meet the Unity boys on some other day, and closed with the following anecdote, to illustrate. A timid boy, the son of his mother, had gained permission to attend the annual military muster, "armed and equipped as the law directs." He took his place in the company, and entered with spirit into the drill exercises of the day. He obeyed all orders of the captain, until he came to the "sham fight," in which each soldier was ordered to "load and fire," when the word was given. He *loaded* every time, until he had inserted twelve charges, but he had not the courage to *fire !* Hence he returned home with his gun loaded to the muzzle. He related to his mother the scenes of the day, and reluctantly exposed his cowardice in omitting to *fire* when ordered. For this the mother rebuked him, and taking the gun "fired it off," to show her own courage. The result was, she was prostrated by the reaction of the overcharged weapon.

The Old District School

Alarmed and trembling, the boy cried out, "Lie still, mother, there are eleven more charges to come yet." Hence it would be prudent for the Unity boys to keep quiet, as there were "eleven" more wrestlers ready for another contest.

In the Clark district school, as I have intimated, the teaching of composition in any form was never attempted. Writing in copy-books was allowed, but not *taught*. In reading, the pupil acquired the habit of uttering improper sounds, mispronouncing words, and the incorrect expression of sentences. In arithmetic, he was required only to "do the sums," without understanding the principles or reasons. It was never suggested that a correct knowledge of this or any other branch of study would be of any practical benefit in the business of life. The study of geography consisted of committing to memory long lists of names and figures, to be forgotten before the next recitation. Grammar was, and continued to be, one of the seven wonders of the world. As a result, the best graduates from this school could not have estimated the measure and value of a pile of wood, could not have expressed correctly a simple sentence, or written a creditable letter to their mothers.

The influence of such a school upon its pupils, and upon the community, was disastrous. There was little in the school or the home calculated to encourage or inspire pupils to seek higher attainments. The condition of families and the community could not make great advancement under such a system of education. Real estate depreciated, enterprise languished, and decay has marked the lapse of time, from generation to generation, in that neighborhood.

This is a fair specimen of the district schools of seventy-five years ago. What a contrast when compared with the schools of to-day! True, the reform has not yet reached all the rural sections of the country. There are still to be found poor schoolhouses, stupid committee men, and unqualified teachers, which indicates a lingering indifference among the people in some localities; but great progress has been made,

during these years, in the cause of education. Vast sums of money are now expended in erecting and furnishing elegant
school buildings, in establishing normal
schools for the education of teachers, and in
providing for the supervision of the schools
of the city, town, and State, and in establishing free libraries, accessible to both parents
and pupils. The district system has been
abolished and the town system substituted
in most of the States. The graded school
has taken the place of the ungraded, and
an excellent system of school management
and improved methods of instruction have
been adopted and are being applied by a
multitude of trained teachers all over the
country. Teachers' associations have been
organized, and are performing a valuable
service in every State in the Union. The
American Institute of Instruction, and the
National Educational Teachers' Association,
numbering thousands of our ablest educators, hold their annual meetings and are leading the educational thought of the nation.

The National Bureau of Education at
Washington, D. C., under the able manage-

ment of Dr. W. T. Harris, successor to General John Eaton, who for sixteen years did excellent work in that important position, is gathering up school statistics for the encouragement and use of educators toiling for still higher attainments in our educational work. And now, more than ever before, our school officers are reaching out into the rural districts for the purpose of bringing these neglected schools under better supervision and instruction. The necessity of universal education for the prosperity of the nation, and the perpetuity of our free institutions, is acknowledged and felt to-day as never before. The improvements made in our educational facilities during the nineteenth century are great and encouraging to our intelligent and patriotic people. But we must not forget that the old district school served its day and generation, and was an essential factor in the process of the evolution of our educational system. And may not the educators of the last quarter of the twentieth century have occasion to find as much fault with our system as we do with that of seventy-five years ago?

II

THE OLD ACADEMY

THE old academy of our boyhood days was the hope of the common school, and the main feeder of the college; but it was necessarily unsystematic, as a result of the irregularity of attendance. Well-arranged courses of study and a graded system of instruction were impossible. Most of the students came from the farm and the workshop, with no preparation except such as they could get in the district school of that day, and they were compelled to work their way unaided. Hence they were obliged to alternate terms of study with terms of labor; to study in the autumn and teach in the winter; to study in the spring and labor in the summer. As a result, the autumn and spring terms were comparatively large, and the winter and summer terms small. Thus proper classification was impossible.

Most of these institutions were unendowed and short-lived, but they were then a necessity. They occupied a position in the educational system of that day which no other school could fill, and performed a work which no other could have accomplished.

The open door of the old academy, its economical arrangements, and its earnest and devoted teachers invited and encouraged the young men and women of the neighborhood to come up higher. It afforded them opportunity for real culture, and directed young men to the college and to the higher walks of professional life. Through the influence and inspiration of these academic institutions of New England, multitudes became better husbands and wives, better farmers, better mechanics, better merchants, better citizens, better teachers, and not a few pressed their way on through a liberal course of study.

Though many of these institutions have done their work and passed away, they should be remembered and honored for what they have accomplished. Graded schools have taken their places, yet a few still enjoy a spasmodic life and serve to kindle "backfires" for the more favored and permanent academies.

The circumstances of my own life were all against gaining access to one of these academies, although I had conceived the idea and cherished the hope that I might sometime be thus favored. Surrounding influences were discouraging, and the necessary means to pay current expenses were wanting. If I took a step in that direction, my success or failure would depend entirely upon myself. How these obstacles could be overcome did not appear, but the crisis in my young life had come, and I must act. I had either to settle down amid the influences by which I was surrounded, or break away from the beaten path which generations of my ancestors had trodden and work my way to something higher and better. I took the risk, and in the autumn of 1834 entered Chester (Vermont) Academy for a single term of three months.

During the next four years, I was struggling to overcome the difficulties which were in the path I had chosen, studying when I could and laboring and teaching when necessary, to earn money to pay my way at school. I was able to study only about half of each of these years, and always under the most discouraging circumstances. These terms of study were at four New England academies, viz.: Chester and Cavendish (Vermont), Kimball Union (New Hampshire), and Phillips Andover (Massachusetts.)

Hallowed associations cluster around these institutions. I recall with intense interest the scenes through which I passed, the fellow-students with whom I mingled, and the principals and assistants under whose instruction I sat. Some of these teachers deserve more than a passing notice. Dr. Taylor, principal of Phillips Andover Academy, was the Arnold of America. As a classical author, as a teacher and disciplinarian, he ranked among the ablest and best in the nation. Dr. Richards, principal of Kimball Union Academy, was a scholarly,

Christian gentleman, a graduate from Dartmouth College, the author of one or two classical text-books, and for many years the head master of that old and honored institution. As a classical teacher he ranked high; as a principal and disciplinarian, though not popular with those who disapproved of his system and method of government, he was eminently successful. Dr. A. A. Miner, assistant teacher at Cavendish Academy, was then a young man of royal presence and fine ability, and, though not a college graduate, he had already distinguished himself both as teacher and preacher. He gained in power and influence, as the years rolled on, became president of Tufts College, and the acknowledged leader of the religious denomination to which he belonged. Professor Wood, assistant teacher at Kimball Union, was a fine scholar — the author of "Wood's Botany," a text-book which was popular in its day — and an able teacher. He was sometimes a little absent-minded, as an example or two will show. One day on returning from a walk, he came to his own office door and knocked for admission, and as no one bade him enter, he returned to the street, forgetting that he had no room-mate, and that he had the key to his door in his own pocket. At another time the professor started from his room, with oil-can in hand, for the store. While on the street, the bell calling to prayers in the chapel began to toll. He turned and started for the academy. Entering the building, doubtless with the impression that he had something about him that he ought not to carry into the audience room, but not realizing exactly what it was, he left his *hat* in the *dust-closet*, and carried his oil-can into the chapel, and placed it on the stage. This ludicrous scene served to make the exercises more cheerful, but probably not more devotional. All these men whom I have mentioned in this connection, and other principals, with their associates who were my teachers, have passed from earth, and but few of their students of that day survive.

III

COLLEGE LIFE

IN the autumn of 1838 I entered Dartmouth College from Phillips Andover Academy, and graduated with my class in 1842. In these new relations as a student, new influences were felt, new ambitions awakened, and new opportunities and facilities were offered and enjoyed.

With the exception of a few academic classmates, all my class and college associates were entire strangers; but we soon became acquainted, and experience taught us that, outside the family, there is no community in which more endearing and lasting friendships are formed than in college. There we met as strangers, but by constant mingling in the dormitories, classroom, and club, we soon came to know and to cherish an abiding interest in each other, in our

college, and in our president and professors.
The mutual friendships formed were more
often among classmates, as our relations to
one another were more intimate. We toiled
and played, enjoyed and suffered together,
day after day and term after term, during
the four short years of college life, and
finally we stood together to receive the
benediction of our president, and bade fare-
well to one another and to the scenes with
which we had become so familiar. We had
treasured up the lessons of these busy
years, the pleasant memories of our honored instructors, and the incidents, songs,
and anecdotes which interested us in these
relations.

Though nearly sixty years have passed
since I left these consecrated halls, and all
the faculty and more than two-thirds of my
classmates have passed away, yet I see them
just as they were, hear their familiar voices,
and live over again, those anxious, hopeful,
and joyful days. I recall my faithful and
scholarly instructors : Professor Haddock,
the refined Christian gentleman who taught
rhetoric and corrected our graduating ora-

tions; Professor Alpheus Crosby, the unassuming but distinguished Greek scholar and
author, our teacher of that elegant language;
Professor Young, the father of the famous
Professor Young of Princeton, a philosopher
and astronomer of marked ability, and a
practical teacher of great skill, — each lesson under him was *normal*, though normal
methods had not then been taught in this
country; Professor Sanborn, the noble man,
our drill-teacher in Latin, and the living
historical encyclopædia of the college, whose
Christian example, energy, and devotion were
a constant inspiration to all who came under
his influence; Professor Brown, a son of
President Brown of the same college, our
teacher in elocution; Professor Chase, the
great mathematician, who presided over our
algebraic, geometrical, and trigonometrical
problems and demonstrations, — he was an
accurate scholar and an earnest teacher,
although less skilled in the management
of young men; and Professor Hubbard,
the chemical genius who revealed to us the
mysteries of acids and alkalies, and demonstrated the facts at every point by unerring

experiments, — after holding his position for many years as chemical professor in the college proper, he was recalled, year after year, to instruct the medical class; our tutors, Messrs. Peaslee, Samuel C. and Joseph Bartlett, — Dr. Peaslee became a distinguished professor in the medical department, and Dr. S. C. Bartlett the president of the college; and finally President Nathan Lord, who presided over Dartmouth College for many years with great ability and skill, and the memory of whose sagacity and alertness in discipline survives in many a good story, which served to relieve the monotony of college life. A few of these anecdotes will illustrate the tone and spirit of college management sixty years ago.

COLLEGE ANECDOTES

As intimated, Dr. Lord was an executive officer of great ability, and he was very popular among the students. Though severe in discipline, he was seldom obliged to punish for malicious insubordination. The fun-loving students sometimes indulged in conduct which required rebuke, for the purpose of enjoying the sport, and to see what the good " Prex " would do about it.

One morning a ram was found in the belfry of the college chapel, tied by his horn to the bell-tongue. Several suspected parties were summoned to the president's office to answer the inquiry, " Can you tell me how that animal got up into the college belfry ? " They had all slept soundly in their own beds through that night, and no one knew anything about the matter, except Mason, who came in last. He answered the question promptly, and said he could give the desired information. " That ram," he said, " climbed up the lightning-rod; I saw his tracks." " That is sufficient, Mason," said the president; " you are excused." Nothing more was ever heard of this case.

At another time, an old lean horse that had been seen grazing by the wayside was found stabled in the chapel, and when the students were coming out from their breakfast, the animal, grotesquely decorated with a large stick attached to his extremity, was let loose and sent down across the common at full speed. Again, students likely to indulge in such irregularities were interviewed by the president. No information, however, could be gleaned, except from one who seemed to understand the case and to be willing to tell all he knew about it. Something like the following was his testimony : "As I issued forth from my dormitory this morning, I spied a quadruped, dressed in uniform, with a beam fastened to his posterior, coming out of the chapel, and he went down over the campus as though his Satanic Majesty impelled him." "But pause," said the president; "your high-flown language is beyond my comprehension. Give me a translation that I can understand." And the witness proceeded to translate as follows : "As I came out of my room this morning, I saw an old horse covered over with pictures, with a rail tied to his tail, and when let loose he ran down over the common as though the devil had kicked him in end." "That will do," said the president, "you are excused."

College Life

A few years later, one of President Lord's faculty was familiarly known as peculiar by his frequent repetition of the expression, "And the converse is equally true." One evening Quint (the late Dr. Quint, so well known as a distinguished clergyman in Massachusetts, and for many years a trustee of the college) and one of his classmates took occasion to "horn" this professor. Unfortunately, President Lord was at that very hour making a call upon his associate, and both gave chase to the horn-blowers, who took flight intentionally in the direction of a deep trench which had recently been dug; and knowing the grounds and being nimble, they cleared the trench at a single leap, but their dignified pursuers fell in! The boys waited developments at a safe distance, listening attentively, and soon heard the professor say, "Now, Dr. Lord, you get on your hands and knees, and I will climb out over you, and then I will pull you out." The Doctor replied, "Yes, yes, but the converse is equally true." A burst of laughter betrayed the boys, when Dr. Lord, recognizing Quint's voice, called

out, "Quint, Quint, come and help us out."
So he did; but the next day the two boys
were called before the president and severely
rebuked for insulting their teachers. "But,"
said Quint to Dr. Lord, "if you had not
made fun of the professor in the trench you
would not have caught us." The president was quick to recognize the keenness
of the reply and let the offenders off easily.

On another occasion, as the story is told,
the president caught a student helping himself to wood from his shed. He arrested
the thief and sternly inquired of him what
authority he had for purloining wood
from his pile. The frightened and mor-
tified student, recalling his Latin syntax,
replied, "Well, sir, 'Opus and usus, signi-
fying *need*, require the ablative.'" The
president responded, "Indeed, you are
then in the ablative case, and in great need!
Take along the wood; you are welcome
to it."

Other cases of discipline illustrate Dr.
Lord's skilful method of management and
his power to control young men. At one
time the chapel Bible from which the presi-

dent was accustomed to read a chapter, in
conducting morning religious services, disappeared. The students had assembled
for prayers, and, having knowledge of the
theft, were keenly interested in the exercise,
expecting to hear a sound lecture on one
of the ten commandments. Soon the
president, not at all disconcerted, rose from
his chair, and standing at his desk, repeated
from memory a psalm with the same readi-
ness and composure as he would have
shown in reading it from the Bible. He
made no allusion to the theft, but his
silence was a more severe rebuke than a
lecture would have been, and before the
next morning the Bible was returned.

At another time, early in the morning,
as we passed into the chapel for prayers,
we were confronted by a frightful black
effigy suspended over the door, reaching
out its arms so as almost to touch our
heads as we walked through the doorway.
All had taken their seats, and the president
was in his desk. A breathless silence prevailed, as we waited to hear what would be
said to rebuke this rowdyism. Nor were

we long in waiting. The president rose in a dignified manner, lifted his glasses to his forehead, and in a distinct voice, and with a pleasing smile, said, " Gentlemen, I perceive that one of our rowdies is suspended." A roar of applause followed. Not another word was spoken upon the subject, but the " rowdies " who committed the offence were not pleased with the company into which the president had introduced them, nor did they hear the last of it from their fellow-students for many a day.

Here is a college pun worth recording. President Lord had eight sons, and all graduated from the college. One of these sons was named Nathan, after his father, and had the reputation of being rather wild and disorderly. Hence the inquiry among the students was, " Why does Dr. Lord believe in ' total depravity ' ? " Answer — " Because it is in-Nate."

Still another college anecdote is worth telling in this connection. Some of the boys had carelessly formed the habit of profanity, but upon reflection were ashamed of it, and resolved to reform. They organized an anti-swearing club, and all signed a pledge which read in substance as follows: " I hereby solemnly pledge that I will not use profane language *anywhere this side of Mink Brook*." This brook, well known to every student and graduate of the college, crosses the highway leading to White River Junction, half a mile more or less from the college.

One morning, very early, a member of this club was seen running with great speed across the campus in a southerly direction. He was hailed by a fellow-student, with the inquiry as to the cause of his haste. With all the gravity of a conscientious man, he replied, " I am going down over Mink Brook to swear. I can't stand it any longer."

INCIDENTS OF COLLEGE LIFE

IT was Saturday night, when a rumor reached the students from the neighborhood of East Hanover, four miles away, that a mother from Pennsylvania had come to Hanover for the purpose of securing the custody of her four boys, then living with their uncle, the brother of her divorced husband. It was stated to us that this intelligent and accomplished woman had learned that her children were not properly cared for, and that she was now able to undertake their future support and education. It was further stated that the uncle had treated her rudely, and sternly refused to give up the children, and that she was in great distress. Our sympathy was awakened, and our indignation aroused. Two of us decided to go at once to the scene of conflict, to aid, if possible, in adjusting matters. We went, and on our return, after spending a full day, reported to the student body. The uncle, who had promised us that he would give up the children, changed his mind, as we soon learned, and swore that he would shoot the next student who came upon his premises. Upon learning this fact, it was at once decided to settle the case without judge or jury. A strong body of students was organized, and carriages secured, for the purpose of taking that mother and her children, by force if need be, and sending

them to her home. This was done with
great ceremony and satisfaction. They
were brought to the college, and money
was raised to pay the expenses of the family
and an accompanying student *en route*,
and they were soon safely settled in-their
Pennsylvania home.

The sequel of the story remains to be
told. Some months later, we were pained
to learn of the death of one of these boys.
The next intelligence received, years afterwards, was that Hon. S. R., an ex-member
of Congress, had died at his home in
Pennsylvania. That honorable gentleman
proved to be the eldest son of that mother
who is the heroine of my story.

I recall with great interest an incident
in which Alpheus Benning Crosby, then a
mere boy, was the actor. He was the son
of Professor Dixi Crosby, for many years
the honored head of the Medical College at
Dartmouth. Young Crosby was a born
physician, and grew up in the very atmosphere of medical life and practice. He
entered college very young, and became a
leader in his class. The incident here to

be recorded will show his maturity, self-possession, and ability. One cold November morning, when the custom was to call in classes for recitation before breakfast, the professor of mathematics, who was in poor health, was seen by the class suddenly to swoon, and, reeling in his chair, to fall heavily forward on his desk. The class seemed paralyzed by alarm, and sat riveted to their seats, all except young Crosby, who was the only *boy* in the class. He at once took in the situation, and, as quickly, knew just what to do. He sprang over the benches, and reached the unconscious professor in time to save him from falling. He removed his collar and cravat from his neck, kicked away the chairs, and laid his master prostrate upon the floor. He ordered the windows opened, and sent one of the " patriarchs " for a glass of water. All his orders were promptly obeyed. Under this heroic treatment the professor soon opened his eyes and recovered consciousness. The young doctor who had taken charge of the case, without waiting to be sent for, now gathered up the scattered effects, brushed the professor's coat, and sent him safely to his home.

As we might expect, we heard from Crosby again. After finishing his college and medical courses, he was soon appointed professor, and later became a leading lecturer before medical classes in *five* different colleges, and had a large practice wherever located. He died in the prime of manhood, while delivering a course of lectures at Dartmouth, and was laid beside his honored father, in the village churchyard.

My Own College Class

THE class of 1842 was the banner class of the college as regards the number of graduates up to date, 1897. We entered one hundred and one; thirty more joined the class during our four years' course; and we graduated eighty-seven. Our average age at graduation was twenty-three, — the youngest was eighteen, and the oldest thirty. The class was physically strong and self-reliant. They could withstand the pressure of sophomore rushes, and one, at least, could hold helpless, at arm's length, any two of their strongest men. One of our boys (who in his manhood was for twenty-five years superintendent of Boston public schools) did attack, single-handed, and repel the "Dartmouth Guards," — a hazing party that had come to his room to insult him, — and drove them away sore-headed.

The class furnished one member to General Grant's Cabinet (Akerman), one distinguished general to the Union Army (Hobart), one governor to the State of Louisiana during the Civil War (Flanders), five judges, — two of whom (Brigham and Nash) were on the Supreme bench in Massachusetts, — one member of the Provincial Parliament in Canada (Sanborn), and several other prominent lawyers. Our physicians ranked high, in practice at home and in the army. Two of them became superintendents of Insane Asylums (Tyler and Walker). Our clergymen have done good service as preachers and pastors, and three of them received the honorary degree of D.D. Our teachers have honored the profession, and some of them gained distinction. Four of the class had conferred upon them the college honor of LL.D.

In June of 1892, seventeen of the thirty-four survivors at that time returned to Dartmouth to celebrate the fiftieth anniversary of our graduation. Time had wrought great changes. We had lost our physical identity. Intimate college friends who had not met for fifty years failed to recognize each other. Why should they, since each of them had seven times exchanged the old for a new body? Death had done its work. Fifty-three of the eighty-seven had died. The average age of those who had died was fifty-six. Ten of this number had attained the age of seventy-three. The average age of the living was seventy-five. Six years later the record stands, sixty-seven dead and twenty living. The class has made a good record and will be remembered.

IV

THE STUDENT BECOMES A SCHOOLMASTER

THE period of my life as a school-master extended over eight years, during which my time was spent in teaching in public schools and in laboring to earn the money necessary to defray the expenses while studying. I taught eight winters in Rockingham and Barre, Vermont, and in Andover and Wellfleet, Massachusetts.

My first little kingdom as a schoolmaster was in the Locke district on Rockingham Hills. I was called to that throne from Chester Academy in 1834, after my first term of academic study. My wages amounted to eleven dollars per month, and board, not among the scholars, but among the *taxpayers*. This method of boarding the schoolmaster was novel even then; but none except crusty old bachelors who had no children to educate found fault with it, and why should they? All property owners in the district always share the expense of the teacher's wages, — and why not the expense of his board as well?

This boarding the teacher around, as in those early days and in a few cases even now, had its advantages as well as disadvantages. The necessity was thus laid upon the teacher to form an intimate acquaintance with all his patrons, and to learn the peculiarities and wishes of each family. This gave him the opportunity to secure their confidence and co-operation, which are absolutely necessary to success, whether he has one or many boarding-places.

On the other hand, there were serious disadvantages in this ancient method of boarding the schoolmaster. He needed the convenience and comforts of a home for rest and study; and really there is no more propriety in boarding the teacher among the taxpayers than in boarding the pastor among his parishioners, or the physician among his patients.

Reminiscences of School Life

My experience in my first school in the Locke district left vivid and lasting impressions on my mind. It was undertaken with peculiar feelings and some misgivings. It seemed a fearful task for a young teacher with only a partial preparation for the work and with no experience. I had charge of forty children, of all ages from four to eighteen years, from every kind of family, representing every phase of human nature. The bright and the stupid, the roguish and the ugly, the restless and the turbulent were all huddled in together, a little world in embryo, and they were here to be governed and taught under the criticism of ignorant and meddlesome fathers and mothers. Never have I achieved a success with more satisfaction and pride than that recognized at the end of my first three months of school-life experience.

The thirty-three dollars in cash, with even the best board which the good mothers of that district could provide, seems inadequate compensation for so much labor, care, and anxiety as were bestowed upon that school. But, in fact, I secured much more than my salary for my services. I gained valuable experience, which was of great use to me in later years. Incessant toil and effort to over-come difficulties gave me strength and con-fidence. I learned how to deal with men, women, and children in their school rela-tions. Finally, I learned human nature, — an important lesson for every schoolmaster, which cannot be learned anywhere else so readily as in a district school. I learned how to manage those parents who were always ready to give advice and to seek special favors for themselves and their children, by listening to them attentively and patiently, without offering offensive opposition, and then acting independently, according to my own judgment, as circumstances required. I found that any attempt to follow such advice and to grant such favors, with a view of pleasing, is to surrender manly independ-ence, and is sure to result in failure.

My second winter school was in Factory Village, Andover, Massachusetts. I found there a very different school, in a very dif-ferent neighborhood from the one I had left in Vermont. The people were largely factory employees and uncultivated, and the children reared in these families differed but little from semi-savages. The village had become missionary ground for the students of Phillips Academy and the Theological Seminary, on Andover Hill. For two years I had been superintendent of a Sabbath-school in this "little red schoolhouse" while a student in the academy. Now I had engaged to teach their district school. The school had run wild for several years, and was regarded as very difficult to manage.

The history of the first few days furnishes an instructive object lesson in school discipline. Indeed the first few days in any school usually determines the teacher's success or failure.

When I entered this school the first morning, the room was filled with pupils, and much confusion prevailed. I rapped upon the desk as a signal for order, and waited until quiet was secured and all were seated. I issued no commands and made no laws, but kept my eyes and ears open, and watched the movements that I might learn the drift of public sentiment and the character and purpose of individual pupils. I began to make inquiries about the studies to be pursued and the text-books to be used, but soon I observed half a dozen boys jumping out of the window and returning through the door. Others left their seats without permission, and chaos seemed again to rule the hour. The question was now to be settled, how to bring the school under control and to hold them under authority. By a special effort I gained their attention and told them I wished to talk to them a few moments, and they seemed ready to listen. I explained to them my position as master and teacher, and their position as pupils, and our mutual relations and duties to each other. I assured them that I was their friend, was interested in their improvement and welfare, and had come to aid them in securing a practical education. To this end, I needed their assistance and co-operation. The school must be orderly, studious, and obedient under necessary rules and regulations; and if they compelled me to secure these results by *force*, I should have but little time to devote to instruction. They seemed interested in my ideas and methods, and appeared ready to express their approval. I then asked all who favored these views, and were ready to pledge obedience and co-operation, to manifest it by rising. By a large majority they voted in the affirmative. I had thus gained complete moral power over them, and had created a favorable public opinion to aid me in my work. I must now check and crush out every act of treachery and insubordination, and this I did promptly and effectually. At the end of the first week, the school was completely organized and under perfect control, and I was able to maintain my position to the end of the term, without resort to severe punishment in many cases. I was urged to re-engage for the next winter, but declined to return.

My third school was in Wellfleet, Massachusetts, on Cape Cod. My conveyance from my home in New Hampshire was by stage, one hundred and fifty miles, to

Boston, and from Boston to the Cape by
sea, in an old fishing schooner, on " Thanks-
giving Day " ! I had not much that day
to be thankful for, seasick as I was, except
that the vessel landed me safely on that
sandy shore. There I found myself in a
different climate, among a " peculiar people." The briny Atlantic that washes the
shore tempers the atmosphere ; and the
bleak winds that sweep over the sandy
plain keep it pure and healthful. People
live their appointed time and die there, as
in other parts of the country, but they
more often live to a good old age or die
a violent death. I remember that there
were in the town of Wellfleet, at the time
I taught school there, sixteen widows
whose husbands had died by drowning.
" Cape Cod Folks," sixty years ago, were
a seafaring people. They then not only
manned a large part of the American fishing
fleet, but also gave officers and sailors to a
large, and possibly the larger part of the
great and world-wide extended merchant
marine of the country. Courage, determination, and business ability were brought

55

out and cultivated by these opportunities
and this kind of life. But there has been
a shrinkage of nearly two-thirds in the
fishing business which, three generations
ago, furnished employment to nearly all
the able-bodied male citizens. Hence
many have turned their attention to agricul-
ture, to growing garden vegetables for the
city markets, and to providing for summer
residents who have learned that Cape Cod
is one of the most desirable summer resorts
in the country. Still they were and are, in
the best sense, a " peculiar people." There
were relatively very few persons residing
among them of foreign birth. In their
manners and habits they were simple and
artless. Their homes were models of peace
and cordiality. In their neighborhood relations they were social and friendly, and always generous and hospitable, to the last
degree, to all who lived among them.
They were an intelligent and religious
people, and manifested much interest in
their schools and teachers. I was treated
with great kindness from the first, and was
furnished the best living that they could

provide. Parents were ever ready to co-operate with me, and to sustain me in the management of their schools.

' My school life in Wellfleet extended over five winters, and in going and coming I had become quite a sailor, having crossed Cape Cod Bay sixteen times. I taught in two districts, — three winters in the " Back Side " district overlooking the broad Atlantic, and two winters in the " Pond Hill " district, in the south part of the town. At the close of my school in the spring, I was each time re-engaged for the next winter.

These schools numbered nearly one hundred pupils each, ranging from six to twenty-five years of age. They were of a decidedly mixed character, and all gathered in one room, to be managed and taught without an assistant! In the " Back Side " school I had a whole ship's crew, including captain, mate, and cook. They had come home from a fishing voyage to spend the winter, and, having nothing else to do, they entered the school. It will be readily seen, as it proved in practice, that the government of such a school was no " boy's play " for the teacher, however much the boys might play.

I propose here to explain the method adopted in the discipline of these schools, as an object lesson. It is expressed by the word *management*. This method includes government based upon authority, yet it aims to avoid the necessity of exercising authority and the infliction of severe punishment. It is based upon the assumption that in the best governed school the controlling power is not visible. That is, the school is so managed that it becomes and remains self-governing. Order is preserved and obedience rendered, yet no visible force is applied to secure the result. There is, indeed, a reserve power behind the throne, which, like the second brake of the engine on the car descending Mount Washington railroad, can be instantly applied in case of an emergency. In applying this method, I always insisted that there could be but one head to my school and that my authority was absolute; yet I planned and labored to secure voluntary conformity to known, necessary rules and regulations. To this end I aimed to gain the confidence of the pupils, large and small, and through them the confidence and co-operation of their parents and friends. But I never failed promptly to check every indication of insubordination and irregularity. The pupils were treated with attention and kindness, at all times and everywhere. Out of school hours I mingled familiarly with them, joined them in their sports, and sympathized with them in all their joys and sorrows. In their homes — where I frequently met them, by the way, — and on the playground we stood on a common level. In the schoolroom, however, I was recognized as master, and so complete was their loyalty — captain, mate and all — that I could punish, if need be, with severity, in the presence of the school, without the least opposition on the part of the offender.

I have spoken of the loyalty of my Cape Cod pupils. I did not mean that they were always careful to observe the rules and regulations of the school. Quite the opposite was true of some of them. They were boiling over with fun, and sometimes enjoyed the novelty of a case of discipline, even at their own expense; but they were always ready to endure the penalty cheerfully.

For example, Seaman Cheever, a large, rough, and good-natured sailor, sat quietly in his seat, studying, as I supposed, "Olney's Geography." He found there a picture representing buffaloes falling into a pit prepared for their capture. In an instant, the quiet of the schoolroom was changed into the utmost confusion by Cheever's boisterous laughter. I at once called him to account, and demanded an explanation. He began to apologize, assuring me that he meant no harm, and went on to say, "Those buffaloes reminded me of the boys jumping off Pond Hill into the snowbank, and I could n't help laughing." I severely rebuked his rude and disorderly conduct, and punished him mildly, as a warning for the school, and he meekly settled down to quiet study.

I had another class of loyal students who aimed to do nothing contrary to law, without permission. Shipmate Swett furnishes an example. He was a young man six feet and two inches tall, of dignified bearing, and occupied a back seat in one corner of the room. He asked permission to speak, which was granted. He rose, and coming down to the front, seated -himself beside a bright little girl, some six years of age, and began conversing with her. His only object was to make fun, and this object was soon accomplished. The ludicrous scene excited great merriment. I was busy in conducting a recitation, but I paused, and, fixing my eyes upon the offender, listened to the conversation. The little girl blushed and manifested great uneasiness. The tall shipmate, taking in the situation, began to realize his own awkward position. I waited the proper time to speak, and then said, " Swett, don't you see how ashamed that little girl appears? " He rose to his feet, and in great confusion marched off to his own seat, amid the convulsive laughter of the school. This treatment of the case was effective and produced a permanent cure.

There were in these schools, as in most

others, a few idle, lawless fellows upon whom moral influence and mild measures had no power. They had no desire for improvement, cared nothing for law and order, had no respect for superiors, and were ready to defy authority whenever it suited their convenience. How to treat this class is a question which every practical teacher has to answer. My own views on this point were formed and expressed many years ago, and my long and varied experience in the discipline of the school has wrought no change in them. We hear much said, in these days, upon the reform method of family and school government. It is maintained by learned theorists in positions of high authority, and it is voted by wise or unwise school boards, that no physical coertion should be allowed in our public schools. If there are children who cannot be controlled by moral suasion, they say, expel them. I say, in answer to these theorists, if they have employed teachers who cannot govern their schools without frequent resort to corporal punishment, turn them out, but allow the skilful disciplina-

The Student Becomes a Schoolmaster

rian to retain the rod for use in such cases as I have described above. It is wrong, it is *cruel*, to turn into the street the stubborn rebellious boy or girl who refuses to be persuaded to submit to authority, and thus give the child over to the officers of the law, soon to be enrolled with the criminal classes. The sensible and humane course is to subdue the rebel by whatever severity necessary, and save him to himself, to his family, and to society. No careful observer has failed to see the evil results of this "milk and water" system of family and school government.

These remarks lead me naturally to describe some hard cases in discipline which have come under my own observation and treatment. I will record them for the benefit of young teachers who may read this page in the history of my experience. I would not be understood, however, as advocating severity as a rule, but only in these exceptional cases. No good disciplinarian often uses violent measures, and when he does, it is not as "a last resort," but as the proper and only remedy for the case in hand. Each case should be treated on its merits, and with a full knowledge of all the circumstances. All hard cases do not require the use of the rod, as the following examples will show.

HARD CASES IN DISCIPLINE.

THE first case I will mention under this head was one of deception followed by defiant rebellion. A large boy had been excused to return home early in the afternoon, on the plea that his father needed his services. I soon discovered him playing ball with friends not members of the school, in sight of the schoolhouse. I immediately sent a messenger to notify him that I ordered him to return at once to school. He refused, and continued his game. Something must now be done, as the school was familiar with all the facts. What should be done, was the question. The boy came to school the next morning, but I did not recognize him as a pupil. He soon discovered by my treatment that he stood suspended until a satisfactory settlement was effected. Later he opened the case in his own behalf, and insisted that he had a right to remain out of school, as he had been excused. I referred him to his false statement when he asked leave of absence, and his refusal to obey my orders to return to school, and gave him a few hours to make a satisfactory confession before the school, and to pledge truthfulness and obedience in the future. If this was not done, I assured him that he would have me to deal with in the final settlement. He came to terms that were satisfactory, and gave me no trouble afterwards.

The next case was still more aggravating and difficult to handle. A bright, talented boy, fifteen years of age, was sent to my academy, with the understanding that he had never been governed at home or in school, and his near relatives expressed doubts as to whether he could be brought under proper school regulations. He had conquered his stepfather in a pitched battle, while *en route*, and the latter did not know what to do with him. I admired the brightness and social qualities of the boy, and became greatly interested in him. But I soon discovered that he had no idea of recognizing me as his master. Still, some time elapsed before we came into conflict.

I was one day conducting a class recitation of which he was a member. Some question was put to him which he answered in an insulting manner. I rose from my chair and stepped down in front of the boy, with no intention of touching him; but he at once assumed a defiant position, which I understood was intended as a challenge to lay hand on him. I accepted it as such, and taking him by the collar I laid him upon his back on the floor. He instantly rose, in great rage, and commenced swearing at me! I did not use the rod upon him, for I had none at hand, but I chastised him severely (taking care not to do him serious injury), and continued to do so until he stopped swearing. I then seated him by my side on the platform, and finished the recitation. He was completely subdued, as I intended he should be, but I had not done with him yet. The most important part of the treatment was yet to come. I must see him *alone*, as I did, and explain to him my feelings and motives in dealing with him so roughly. This was exactly the time when moral suasion could be brought to bear upon him to some purpose. I talked to him in the tone and spirit of a friend, and he recognized me as such, told me frankly, and told others who had come to sympathize with him and take his part against me, that I was right and he was wrong ; and years afterwards, when I met him, he said that my treatment of him on that occasion was of great value to him in after life. He became a successful business man, and remained a warm personal friend to the day of his death.

The next case I will describe reveals a method of dealing with moral evil in school. A boy of twelve years of age was known in my academy as an active, good-natured, and social little fellow, but circumstances awakened suspicion that he might be, with all, " light-fingered." Subsequent events confirmed this suspicion, and when a sum of money, in bills, had disappeared from the teacher's drawer, there remained no doubt that this boy had it. After full investigation, I decided upon a course of treatment of the case. At morning prayers I called the attention of the school to the facts, told them that the thief was one of their number and was present, that I saw in his nervous excitement not only evidence of his guilt, but of the consciousness that he had made a great mistake, and would gladly make restitution if he could have the opportunity. I then described the nature of the crime, and spoke of the personal disgrace and the mortification of friends that would result from public exposure. Now, to save the guilty party from these consequences, I proposed to him a way of escape. I said, if I found the stolen money in my chapel Bible the next morning, I should regard the fact as full evidence that he had sincerely repented of his sinful act, and would not expose him. All this time the little culprit was evidently in agony, and anxious to hide himself from public view. The next morning, on the re-assembling of the school, I found the identical bills carefully laid in the Bible, as I had suggested. The announcement to the school produced a pleasant sensation, but no one appeared so delighted as the boy himself. I now took occasion to commend the acts of repentance and restitution, and to impress the lesson upon the hearts of the pupils. Thus ended the whole affair, and happy results followed, as seen in the correct and successful business life of the man who had been an erring boy.

Another case, sad and troublesome, was treated in the same academy. The conduct of two young men required unconditional separation from the school. I asked no advice, but told them that they must leave. There were yet no demonstrations of sympathy on the part of the student body, but I knew there would be, if nothing was done to forestall it. Hence I called up the matter before the school, and expressed my grief in being compelled to pronounce the sentence upon the young men, and my sympathy for them. Though this verdict could not be changed, yet I was ready to do anything in my power in the future for their welfare. I told my students that I wanted an expression of their approval of my action, if they could approve, and called for a standing vote. Every one in the hall, including the expelled young men, instantly rose to sustain me. I had now gained a moral victory. All had committed themselves, and could not make me trouble in the future, however much they might sympathize with their unfortunate companions. I did not ask the school *what* I should do under the circumstances. That was for me to settle. I asked them to approve my action, as I knew they would. Had I doubted this, I should not have put the vote. My motive was to fix public opinion in favor of correct deportment and good order.

Still another case was treated later. A young girl of fifteen summers had been sent to my Ladies' Seminary. She had never been governed at home, and she was not at all disposed to recognize authority or submit to dictation in school. Her mother told me frankly, that if the child could not be persuaded, it was better to allow her to conquer than to *force* obedience, but *she wanted me to control her!* The girl was a member of the instrumental music class, and one of the requirements was that each scholar should practise her lesson upon the piano a certain number of hours each day. One afternoon it was reported to me that this young lady had refused to practise. I took her in hand, and ordered her to obey her teacher, and conform to the rules of the school. Again she refused, but gave no reason for her action. I insisted, and remained by her side at the piano, waiting for her to obey my order, from early evening to nearly midnight. She submitted, and I was again master of my school. Had this rebellious student been a boy, the question would have been settled in fifteen minutes, but "circumstances alter cases."

The last specimen case of discipline which I will record was peculiar, but it is liable to occur in the experience of any teacher; hence I will state the circumstances and my method of treatment. An angry mother had the impression that her son had been ill-treated, and with more valor than discretion had come to the school, in school hours, to give the schoolmaster a lecture! She came in without knocking, and began in an excited manner to scold me. I told her that I had no time, and that the schoolroom in school hours was no place to discuss the matter; that if she would be seated and remain until the school was dismissed I would talk with her, or if she would retire I would see her at her home the first opportunity. This proposition did not satisfy her. For a moment she insisted upon her right to talk to me then and there. But seeing that I was about to enforce my orders, she became quiet and left. In due time, a conference was held, and the difficulty settled to our mutual satisfaction. These six examples of "hard cases" in school discipline serve to show different methods of treatment, as each differs from every other and may have many duplicates in the experience of readers of these pages.

The Student Becomes a Schoolmaster

I LEFT Cape Cod at the close of my fifth winter with sincere regret. I had become very much attached to my loyal pupils and the kind-hearted people whom I had known so long and so well.

After my return from the Cape for the last time, and from the hayfield where I had spent my summer vacation, I was taken down with fever, and was for some weeks under Professor Dixi Crosby's medical care. I had begun to recover, but had gained hardly strength enough to walk from my room to the carriage in the street when I had a call to Barre, Vermont, to finish a term of select school which had been begun by a young man who had just received an appointment as a cadet at West Point. I accepted the offer, and hastened to the scene of my labors. I found it a new position and very difficult to fill, but was able to carry the burden through with a good degree of satisfaction. In the mean time, the district committee prevailed upon.

73

me to engage to teach the public school in the same district, the winter term. This was my last term of service in the district school. It was a large and very difficult school to govern. It differed from my other schools, not so much in the fun-loving propensity of the pupils as in the character of the lawless actions of the pupils, many of whom were stubborn and malicious. I never found fault with mere playfulness and roguery, if the pupil was respectful and loyal; but the wilful rebel who defied authority and broke every rule that came in his way found in me a hard but faithful master. I did not expel, but subdued him, and then treated him with attention and kindness, and I seldom if ever failed to make him my friend. I had more such pupils to manage in Barre than in Wellfleet, but I was able to carry the school through successfully. I then returned to college, at the opening of the spring term, to resume my studies, and to complete the year's work in less than six months, as I had already lost two terms of that year.

The Student Becomes a Schoolmaster

I had now taught district schools eight terms of three months each, and one select school two months. I had still one year more to complete my college course, but only half of this year could be spent with my class. I was engaged during the fall term of 1841 as associate principal of Hebron (New Hampshire) Academy, under Mr. Leonard Tenny, a college mate, an associate as a Cape Cod schoolmaster, and a life-long friend, and during the winter I was principal of the same academy. Here I had less discipline, but more instruction in higher branches, which proved to be a new experience of great value in my subsequent academic life. I was brought in contact with more mature minds, with ambitious, scholarly, and critical young men and women who came into my classes, several of whom became distinguished in after life. In the spring of 1842, I returned to Dartmouth to spend my last terms of study and to graduate. The goal was finally reached, and the object of my ambition attained, though imperfectly; but rough was the road and desperate the effort necessary to gain it. Not half of the first four years in the preparatory course, as I have stated, had I been able to spend in study, and only ten of the sixteen terms in college could I remain with my class.

THE PROFIT AND LOSS ESTIMATED

A BRIEF review of this struggle and its results seems appropriate in this connection. My education cost me eight years of time and of hard work, and all the money I could earn by manual labor and teaching, and four hundred dollars for which I was in debt when I graduated. And I sold my watch on commencement day to Professor Cyrus Baldwin of Kimball Union Academy for forty dollars, to enable me to meet my share of class expenses and make a contribution to the college library.

Another question arises here, — Was it wise to make this sacrifice and contract a debt at the risk of future success? My answer is, I have never regretted my course in this regard, but rather that I did not secure an additional loan and spend two or three years more, at least, in supplementary study in the university and normal school. It would have added much to my efficiency as a teacher and to the certainty of success.

I have no sympathy with the false notion that a collegiate education is not a desirable preparation for professional study, and I have no respect for the false guide who would advise a young man, because he is poor, to pass by the college and rush into the profession of law, medicine, teaching, or the ministry with no preparation, except to learn his trade as does the blacksmith or the carpenter. The preparatory discipline of the college, in addition to the professional, is in every case desirable, if the candidate would make the most of himself and his opportunities. If he has wise counsellors, the ambitious young man, though entirely dependent, will seek the discipline and culture of as thorough an academic and collegiate course as is within his reach and attainable means, before he enters upon his professional studies or the business of his life. He needs first and most of all the attainment of intellectual manhood, what-

ever is to be his future position and work.
The lamented Dr. Miner, while he was
president of Tufts College, and at the same
time one of the leading preachers and pastors in the city of Boston, when he came
to New Hampshire to deliver a lecture
before my school, remarked to me that he
had always regretted his decision to enter
professional life while yet so young, and without more careful preparation. He said:
"Had I realized the possibilities of life,
I should have taken a thorough collegiate
course." Yet Dr. Miner was a poor boy
and entirely dependent upon himself, and
his regret was expressed with this fact fully
in view. And many others, under similar
circumstances, have felt and spoken in the
same way,—but who ever heard a successful professional man who had enjoyed the
advantages of a liberal education regret
that he had spent so much time and money
in academic and collegiate study? Still, we
are told that very many of our most distinguished men in public life have gained
their positions without college training.
But even these exceptions do not militate

The Student Becomes a Schoolmaster

against liberal culture, as Dr. Miner's case plainly shows. If they have done so much and so well without the advantages of systematic instruction, they would have done more and better with them.

Too long our professional schools have held a rank hardly above that of trade schools, and have been producing physicians who are nothing but physicians, lawyers who are nothing but lawyers, and clergymen who are nothing but clergymen, — men capable of devotion to merely a single branch of knowledge. It is an encouraging fact that there is an increasing determination among our leading educators to improve professional training, and especially to demand the acquisition of that general knowledge which makes a truly cultivated man a prerequisite to professional study.

But the main question returns for a more detailed answer, — What was lost and gained in consequence of my "straightened circumstances?" The fact that I was entirely dependent upon myself cost me more time in preparing for college. I suffered on the score of health from irregular habits of living, — self and club boarding. I lost the benefit of careful and systematic study, and consequently class standing in scholarship, which I might have held, if I could have had the same opportunity that many of my classmates enjoyed.

On the other hand, I gained physical vigor from the necessity of manual labor, and lasting benefits from contact with the busy world, and, with all, I acquired the habits of self-reliance, industry, and economy, without which success in life is impossible. Dr. Cable has told us that "hard experiences are often the foundation stones of a successful life."

I pause right here to make a confession of an absolute failure when preparing for college at Kimball Union Academy, — the only *complete* failure that I am willing to acknowledge in my busy life. This resulted from an effort to bake a johnny-cake on a box-stove in an open dish. The meal was mixed with water all right, but the baking was a failure for causes then beyond my knowledge or control. And my loss of time, all the capital invested, and my supper, were irrecoverable. The cooking teacher was not then " abroad."

Now I may refer to the balance-sheet in the ledger of poverty and wealth. How stands the account between the poor and the wealthy student who have pursued and completed a course of study side by side, and passed out into the world for another trial of ability and strength? Success certainly crowns the life of the poor student, who worked his way, as frequently as that of the rich who was carried through his course of study. The history of every college in the nation, and the experience and observation of living men in active life, confirm this view of the question.

There is one more item of the account which has not been placed upon the balance-sheet; namely, the gain resulting from having broken away from the influences by which my boyhood was surrounded, to pursue a course of study, imperfect as it was. That it was a gain and not a loss, I have only to compare the results to myself, my family, and the world, with those of many of my early companions, of at least equal ability and means, who remained at home. An education, however much it may have cost, if properly used, always pays with good interest on the investment; and the more thorough and extensive, the more valuable it is.

V

THE SCHOOLMASTER BECOMES
A PRECEPTOR.

BEFORE leaving college, I had accepted an appointment by the trustees of Hebron Academy as their principal. I had already taught there, as an associate principal and principal, for two terms, as before stated ; now I was to take charge of the school, to begin in the autumn of that year. This was one of those new-born and short-lived academies which accomplished much for the cause of education in their day. Among the trustees was the distinguished Colonel Berry, who became the war governor of New Hampshire in 1861–62, and lived to be nearly ninety-eight years of age. The school opened in September, 1842, with encouraging prospects. Among my pupils was Austin F. Pike, who recited to me his last academic lesson in the academy, and at once entered upon the study of law with Judge Nesmith of Franklin, became a leading lawyer in the State, speaker of the House of Representatives, and United States Senator.

Soon after accepting this position, I married Miss Sarah A. Cummings of Andover, Mass. She acted as preceptress in this and other schools, and in the care of our large family of pupils, with marked ability and fidelity for twenty-one years, to the day of her death, and she contributed largely to my success. It was not our purpose to make Hebron our permanent home, and we were not long in waiting for a change. About the middle of the winter term, Messrs. Short, Latham, and Howard, three prominent men of Thetford, Vermont, and trustees of Thetford Academy, called upon us, spent the night, and looked up our record in the school and neighborhood, and before leaving informed me that I was elected principal of their academy. After some investigation, I accepted, to begin in April, 1843. This gave us but two terms at Hebron.

Thetford Academy

Thetford Academy is one of the oldest institutions of its kind in New England, having been founded in 1819. Among its founders and most influential early trustees was the famous Dr. Asa Burton, the great theologian of his day. He was the author of the "Taste Scheme," as it was called, in distinction from the "Exercise Scheme" as held by Dr. Emmons of Franklin, Mass. These two theological leaders engaged in a long and animated discussion on this subject; the one maintaining that a man's taste (or disposition) constituted him saint or sinner, though it remain dormant; the other claiming that there could be no holiness or sin unless this disposition is exercised. Dr. Burton was pastor of Thetford village church for more than fifty years.

I recall with deep interest the board of trustees who served in that office during my administration. They were able, wise, and public-spirited men, always ready to sustain and aid their principal every way in their power. The board consisted of Hon. Simeon Short, Rev. E. G. Babcock, Rev. Erdix Tenney of Lyme, N. H., Prof. Ira Young, and Prof. Alpheus Crosby of Dartmouth College, Dr. Nathaniel White, Dr. E. C. Worcester, Abijah Howard, Esq., and Enoch Slade, Esq. I would not fail to recognize the intelligent and hospitable citizens and their families in that neighborhood who contributed cheer and relief to our careworn lives by their kind words and social entertainments.

In alluding to the two pastors of the old church on Thetford Hill, and their connection with the academy, I will mention that soon after we were settled at Thetford, I wrote, by request of the editors, a series of articles for the "Congregational Journal," published at Concord, N. H., on the life and character of Dr. Burton, which led me to investigate and to measure his immense power and great influence over that community. Rev. Mr. Babcock, our pastor, was a strong man and an able writer, but not a pulpit orator. He had formed one peculiar habit in his study, which had great power over him. He always wrote in full his sermons for each Sabbath service, and read them with great rapidity. These sermons were always written between Friday noon and the hour when they were to be delivered. He told me that he could write them at no other time.

The academy which was now to come under my management, and for the success of which I was to be responsible for the next twelve years, had run very low under its former principal. He had already left town, and the last term of the year was in charge of Judge S. Short, one of the trustees, and numbered but thirty-two students, — boys and girls gathered from the immediate neighborhood.

On surveying the ground, I understood the situation. The old academy building, worth perhaps $500, was the only property held in trust by the trustees. The school had to be supported by a low-rate tuition. The capacity of the village to accommodate students from abroad was limited. But this was not the time to worry about insufficient accommodations;

for the school to be accommodated was not in sight. The outlook was not encouraging, nor calculated to awaken large expectations or great enthusiasm. But we had come to stay for several years, and I settled down upon the purpose to win success by earnest, persistent toil, if success were possible. I arranged to open the fall term with a full board of teachers, and a course of study, both classical and English, sufficient to fit for college and for business. I sent out my circulars broadcast, and very soon there appeared another circular, almost an exact copy of mine, except the names, announcing a select school, to begin at the same time, at Post Mills (a village in the same town, two miles away). I had promised lectures from abroad to be delivered to my school. The Post Mills echo circular repeated, without quotation marks, *lectures from abroad.* This school was designed as a rival to Thetford Academy, but it did not prove very discouraging. Our terms opened, and the roll-call showed one hundred and four students at Thetford, and about thirty at Post Mills; and as the

Schoolmaster Becomes a Preceptor

term progressed, the flood-tide seemed to
be running my way. I was the only
lecturer "from abroad" secured at Post
Mills. That school broke up at the end
of the term, and most of the students
entered my school when it next opened.
There was now no rival academy nearer
than Kimball Union, at Meriden on the
south, and St. Johnsbury Academy on the
north.

The winter and summer terms were
always smaller than the fall and spring
terms, but the school continued to increase each corresponding term of the year,
until the village was literally packed, and
every available spare room was occupied by
students. The attempt was now made to
expand. Burton Hall, named after Dr.
Burton, was erected on the north side of
the academy, to furnish rooms for young
men; and " Mrs. Burton Hall,"on the south
side, to furnish rooms for young women.
Four dormitories were finished off in the
attic of the academy. This mention re-
calls the history of the short life of a
remarkable young man who was then one

89

of my students, — David Conant from Lyme, N. H., the brother of Judge C. C. Conant of Greenfield, Mass. He was a mechanic. He undertook the building of these rooms. He drove the ox-team which drew the lumber, and himself, alone, constructed the rooms, thus earning so much toward defraying his expenses in school. We will follow Conant a little further. He finished his academic studies, and entered the Medical College at Hanover, from which he graduated in due time, soon gained a large practice in New York City, and was, when he died, a professor and lecturer in several medical colleges. He died early, of a malignant disease contracted in his practice.

Our additional rooms were soon filled, and we were more than ever in need of still better accommodations. Each announcement in the papers that the village was full brought a new stage load of applicants for admission. These were domiciled in the suburbs, even at some distance from the academy. The school continued to increase until two hundred and fifty-two were enrolled and on the ground at the same time, packing the boarding-houses to repletion. In 1850, four hundred and thirty-six different students entered the academy from fifteen states. At that time, half-fare railroad tickets to and from Thetford could be bought at the depots in Boston and Worcester, Mass.

I had increased my board of instruction, expanded and perfected the courses of study, and organized regular classes for graduation, both classical and English. At the close of the second year, and ever afterwards, large classes graduated and entered college, or pursued the business of active life. During the twelve years, one hundred and thirty-three young men entered Dartmouth, Harvard, Yale, Amherst, Williams, Brown, Middlebury, Tufts, and Vermont University, and nearly all of them graduated in due time. Quite a number of young ladies, and some young men, from these classes entered upon the profession of teaching as their life-work. The number of students enrolled in Thetford Academy during my administration was more than twenty-five hundred.

Reminiscences of School Life

I cherish an affectionate and grateful remembrance of the forty-eight associates and assistant teachers employed in Thetford Academy during this period. We always worked together in perfect harmony.

My labors at Thetford Academy were incessant. I had the entire financial business of the school to conduct without a clerk; the management and discipline of the school, the oversight of every department of instruction, and taught classes myself, from six to seven hours per day, five days per week. Added to this, and an occasional lecture before the school, was the labor of conducting a Bible class, consisting of the whole school, Sabbath morning; a class of young men at noon, in the church; of attending two church services during the day, and a social religious meeting in the academy in the evening, in which I usually took part. And even this was not all. I had reason to expect a call at any time, at unseasonable hours, to some boarding-house or store to quell a disturbance or settle a dispute.

Vacations were a welcome *change*, but no

Schoolmaster Becomes a Preceptor

relief from toil and care. A new school must then be gathered, and arrangements made for the ensuing term. This was my work, my care, and my responsibility, without cessation, during the entire twelve years. Yet, though excessive, I did not regard it as a burden that could not be borne. I fully realized that " eternal vigilance " and hard labor are the price of success. Were I again placed in the same position, however, with my present views, I should devote more hours, especially on the Sabbath, to rest or recreation.

THETFORD ACADEMY SEVENTY-FIFTH ANNIVERSARY

THE memory of that throng of students who gathered on Thetford Hill during the eventful years of my administration as the head of the old academy has always been pleasant and inspiring; but this feeling was greatly intensified by attending the seventy-fifth anniversary of its life in June, 1894. I was invited to return to review the scenes of my former labors, and to meet my old students, many of whom I had not seen for forty or fifty years. I expected to meet them, but the *young* men and women who in the days of our school life recognized me as their preceptor were not there. Only their representatives had come to the anniversary.

The ringing of the old academy bell called to a reception in the hall where, half a century ago, we were accustomed to assemble daily. I answered the call, and was greeted at the door by scores of people who claimed to know me, but many of whom I did not recognize. I pressed my way into the chapel. Every seat and all the standing room were occupied. They rose to greet their old preceptor, not the earnest and loyal students I used to meet there, but careworn and hoary-headed men and women. They bore the same names, unless they had been changed by marriage, and claimed identity; but I could not recall them.

On the platform were seated several of my former associate teachers, and by the table stood the presiding officer of the occasion. It was not John Eaton, the noble, unassuming, and faithful young man who used to come to me for instruction and counsel, but General John Eaton, LL.D., from Washington, D. C., a man of national reputation, gained by his official connection with the government during the Civil War, his sixteen years of service at the head of the National Bureau of Education, and the ex-president of Marietta College. Later we were called to the village church, which was filled to overflowing, to listen to the historic address and poem prepared for the occasion. The genial general was the presiding officer there also, as at the morning session. It had been announced that the address would be delivered by Carlos Slafter, and the poem by Edward A. Jenks; but this was a mistake. These gentlemen were Rev. Professor Carlos Slafter, who had been forty years the honored principal of Dedham (Mass.) High School, and Hon. Edward A. Jenks, A.M., the scholarly gentleman and successful business man from Concord, N. H.

Again, in the evening, we repaired to the church for another session, to be presided over by Chester C. Conant, and addressed by Thomas W. Bicknell, and others. But the presiding officer was Judge Chester C. Conant of Greenfield, Mass., and the address was by Hon. Thomas W. Bicknell, LL.D., of Providence, R. I. In the afternoon we were invited to the large tent on the Common, to partake of a sumptuous dinner, and to listen to the after-dinner speeches. There Dr. Bicknell appeared, presiding at the tables. He had grown so tall since he left the old academy, as a student, that he hardly knew whether he lived on earth or in the heavens. His preceptor, in his after-dinner speech, gave as a reason for his altitude that he was reared in Rhode Island, a State so small that he could grow only in one direction, and that his baldness might be due to the fact that his head reached beyond the region of vegetation. Among the speakers at the table were Hon. Henry Albert Morrill, LL.D., professor in the Cincinnati (Ohio) Law School; Rev. Alva Hovey, D.D., president of the Theological

Schoolmaster Becomes a Preceptor

Seminary at Newton Centre, Mass.; Judge
C. C. Conant, Hon. Gilbert E. Hood, and
Rev. Wm. S. Palmer, D.D. These were
all former students in Thetford Academy,
but now, with many others present and
absent whom they represented in the
different professions and honorable avoca-
tions, are among the foremost men in the
life of the nation. They had come back to
tell us what the young men who gathered
for instruction in these consecrated halls,
during this peroid of the school's history,
had accomplished in the world. It may
here be safely claimed, that no academy in
the nation, in the same length of time, ever
graduated an abler, better, and more successful class of students.

The lawyers present at the anniversary
represented Judge Gleason of Thetford,
trustee of the academy; Hon. A. W.
Tenney of Brooklyn, N. Y., United States
district attorney and judge and orator at
General Grant's tomb on memorial day
last year; Hon. Lyman Hinckley, late
Lieutenant Governor of Vermont; Hon.
H. J. Boardman, president of the Massa-

chusetts Senate for two years; Judge J. B. Richardson, of the Supreme Court in Boston; Hon. A. S. Marshall, district attorney for New Hampshire; Hon. Ira Colby of Claremont, N. H., and many others worthy of honorable mention.

The physicians present represented such men in the profession as Prof. C. P. Frost, LL.D., for many years at the head of the Medical College at Dartmouth College; Dr. Wm. L. Worcester, an expert physician for mental diseases and an able writer on medical subjects; Dr. Osgood Mason of New York City; and many other able practitioners.

The clergymen present represented Rev. Gustavus D. Pike, D.D., of the American Missionary Association; Rev. Wilson A. Farnsworth, D.D., for more than forty years a leading missionary in Turkey; Rev. Alfred Putnam, D.D.; Rev. George W. Gardner, D.D.; Rev. Calvin C. Hulbert, D.D.; and a score of other able preachers and pastors.

The teachers present represented three college presidents, — General Eaton, Dr.

Gardner, and Dr. Hulbert; at least three college professors, — Professor Ruggles of Dartmouth, Professor Woodworth of North Dakota University, and Professor Perry of Williams College, a distinguished author and the champion of Free Trade, who was once pitted against Horace Greeley in a public discussion on that subject. The last time I met Professor Perry, he spoke with much earnestness upon his favorite subject, alluding sneeringly to "a duty on hides," which was then, as more recently, under discussion in Congress. I said to him that he doubtless knew more than I did upon this disputed question, but one thing I did know, I performed my duty on hides while he was my pupil, and to this he might owe his success in life. Hon. Gilbert E. Hood, my honored successor as principal of Thetford Academy; Hon. Edward Conant, for six years state superintendent of public instruction, and now principal of a Vermont Normal School; Hon. Frederick Bates, superintendent of schools and Mayor of Titusville, Pa.; Prof. George C. Mack, Prof. Henry

Babcock, and Prof. S. W. Burnham of the Chicago University, are also among the distinguished professional teachers educated at Thetford Academy during these years.

The old academy also shared in the sacrifices and honors of the Civil War. General Eaton gained his title by his official connection with the Union Army; among others who went to the front were Gen. Charles E. Hovey, Gen. John B. Sanborn, Majors E. W. and E. P. Farr, Col. S. A. Adams, Captains George Farr, T. Sanborn, and Edwin B. Frost, surgeons, Prof. C. P. Frost, Doctors H. H. Gilbert, G. M. Eaton, and R. O. Mason. General Hovey was severely wounded, and Captain Frost was shot dead on the battlefield while acting as major.

This anniversary recalled the names and deeds of many wives, mothers, and teachers who were my pupils at Thetford Academy. They too, as equals of the young men with whom they were associated as students, in scholarship, fidelity, and loyalty, deserve honorable mention.   Mrs. Mary (Clemant)

Schoolmaster Becomes a Preceptor

Leavitt, of Hilo, Hawaii, leads this noble band. She was sixty-three years old, she said, and the last eleven years she had travelled 160,000 miles, sailed in 114 steamers, written 32,564 pages, held 2,301 meetings, employed 252 interpreters to change words into 47 different languages, and formed 140 societies. All this time she travelled alone. She devoted fifteen years to missionary work without compensation, except her living and necessary expenses; organizing, teaching, and lecturing in thirty-five different countries. Two of her three daughters are prominent teachers in the United States, and the third is the mother of her three grandchildren. Twenty-five other representative wives and mothers of distinguished merit, most of whom were teachers before their marriage, might here be named, if space would allow, and a score of single lady teachers, five of whom have been missionaries in foreign lands. In this allusion to my former pupils in this academy, I have coupled the living with the dead. Each class deserves equal recognition and affectionate remembrance.

Reminiscences of School Life

" The joy of meeting not unmixed with pain.
Where are the others ?   Voices from the deep
Caverns of darkness answer me, ' They sleep.'
I name no names ; instinctively I feel
Each at some well-remembered grave will kneel,
And from the inscription wipe the weeds and moss,
For every heart best knoweth its own loss.
I see their scattered gravestones gleaming white
Through the pale dusk of the impending night ;
O'er all alike the impartial sunset throws
Its golden lilies mingled with the rose ;
We give to each a tender thought, and pass
Out of the graveyards with their tangled grass,
Unto those scenes frequented by our feet
When we were young and life was fresh and sweet."

Never was there a better, more faithful
and loyal class of students in one body than
were among the two thousand five hundred
who were under our care at Thetford Academy.   Some manifested boyish propensities
and indulged in boyish tricks, but very few
were ever guilty of wilful insubordination.
Of two or three exceptions I have spoken
in another connection.   One of the loyal
rogues told me, twenty years afterwards,
that I should not have caught him in Par-
son Babcock's dooryard blowing a horn if

Schoolmaster Becomes a Preceptor

I had not worn another man's hat and carried in my hand a horn captured from another fellow. A second one was caught carrying eggs and dishes from the store to his room, preparatory to a night supper, which he knew was not allowed. He was required to deposit the articles in my office for the night, and the next morning, in the presence of all observers, to return them to the store where they were purchased. At the breakfast-table this young man remarked to his fellow-students that "he should have to keep a hen in his room to lay eggs, as it cost too much to pass them through the custom-house." Still another rogue bore patiently the mortification of exposure of the fact that I had pulled him out from under a bed where he had attempted to hide himself from my presence, leaving his hat and one shoe as silent witnesses of his guilt. But cases like these were only episodes in the routine of a pleasant school life. It was our aim in this and all our other schools to bring students under the influence of Christian principles, and to guide them in the duties of the

Christian life : to inspire as well as to teach ; to make men and women worthy of honor, and qualified for usefulness in their day and generation.

The question here arises, Why should we, or why did we, think of leaving Thetford Academy, since we had been there so long, and were so favorably settled? We had no such purpose in mind, long before the decision was made. I had refused two earnest calls to the principalship of other schools, — one a new academy at Oxford, N. H., and the other a ladies' seminary at Orange, N. J. But with all the kindness and co-operation proffered us by the trustees and leading citizens in the community at Thetford, we were much annoyed by the frequent collisions between another class of citizens and our students. A large school gathered from town and city always contains some roguish young fellows who enjoy boyish tricks. Though they mean no serious harm, they want to see what will be done about it, when they remove sign-boards from their places on the cross-roads to the entrance of some dooryards, or hang

some gate taken from a garden fence across
the highway, or remove the tongue from
the village church bell on Saturday night.
And these rogues always seek to annoy
those citizens who have the least judgment
in dealing with such cases. Irritated by
such offences, which are always charged to
the students, with or without evidence,
these citizens become very much enraged,
and declare the academy in town a nuisance,
and prosecute a religious warfare upon
the suspected parties.

A case to illustrate is fresh in mind.
One of these citizens and a student chanced
to meet at the store. A controversy arose
between them. The student had stepped
upon the citizen's toes on a previous occasion. The citizen threw the student into
the wood-box. The student rallied, and,
seizing a burning lamp from the counter,
threw it against the citizen's head, inflicting
a wound which required surgical treatment.
The student sent for his principal, acknowledged to him the wrong he had done, and
expressed a willingness to do anything
that he decided just and proper to make

restitution. But the injured citizen would listen to no settlement by agreement or arbitration. The offender must be prosecuted. I urged a settlement by arbitration, and pledged that the young man should abide by the judgment, but to no effect. I then said, "Proceed with your prosecution. I shall defend and protect my student." But when the sheriff came for his prisoner, he was not there, but in another State, on his way home! I was very much disgusted and exhausted, and on going to my room, near midnight, found among my letters which came in the last mail, a call to take the principalship of North Granville (N. Y.) Ladies' Seminary. I at once replied, favoring the proposition, and promised to make a visit to investigate. The result was the acceptance of the call and a resignation of my position at Thetford. There probably had been no day before, during the twelve years of my life at Thetford, when I should have considered this call favorably. But the die was cast, and the change had to be made. The announcement created much excitement in the school and neighborhood, and many strong expressions of regret followed, even by those who had made all the trouble.

INCIDENTAL OCCURRENCES

I HERE recall two or three incidents which occurred during this period of my school life worthy of note in this connection. On accepting the position as principal of Thetford Academy, I found myself within twenty-five miles of Kimball Union Academy, and Dr. R., my old preceptor, was still in charge. Our schools now came into sharp competition for patronage. Thetford at this time quite equalled Kimball Union in numbers, and although our boys could not afford the time and money for the additional year of preparatory study required there, as many entered Dartmouth, each year for several years, from my school as from his, and when graduating they shared equally the college honors. These facts were naturally distasteful to the good Doctor, and he did not hesitate to express his astonishment and views upon the subject. This rivalry between the two principals became contagious, and was shared by the students, and the two schools were brought into collision. The class from each school, on entering college, maintained its loyalty and strove to excel its rival. Kimball Union Academy had long been under Dr. R.'s management, while the principal of Thetford Academy had recently taken charge of that institution. The system of government adopted at Thetford was radically different from that in vogue at Kimball Union, and as unchangeable as the laws of the " Medes and Persians." Both were mixed schools. The young women boarded in the same families and recited in the same classes with the young men. At Thetford the aim of the principal was to allow them to mingle socially under proper regulations and restraints, while at Kimball Union they were forbidden to mingle socially. The purpose of the one was to *regulate* their intercourse; that of the other, entirely to *separate* them, except when at meals or in the classroom. The result of these two methods of treatment tested the merits of each. In the one case, quiet and good order prevailed, and no case of gross impropriety ever occurred. In the other, constant irritation and law-breaking brought the students into conflict with the principal, and secret interviews, walks, and rides were planned and executed. If they were caught the offenders suffered severe punishment. Cases might be cited to illustrate. The question of mixed or separate schools, which is the better system? is not raised here, but — How shall the *mixed* academy be managed?

While in charge of Thetford Academy, I was accustomed to invite distinguished lecturers from abroad to address my school. I had invited Mr. Justin Morrill — then a bright young man living in Strafford, but since, for thirty-seven years and now at the age of eighty-eight, an able and honored member of the United States Senate from Vermont — to deliver a lecture. In this case, it was an exchange. In compensation for his lecture, I lectured before his village Lyceum. I remember when he was introduced to the audience, he began by saying that he had heard of a clergyman claiming for himself only moderate ability, who, on exchange of pulpits, always brought a peck of beans to pay the balance. He expressed regret that he had forgotten his beans. I have spoken with high commendation and great interest of our Thetford trustees, of the intelligence and culture of the leading citizens and their families in that neighborhood, and of their cordiality towards us, their principals, and interest in our school. But every village, like every circus, has its clown, and we had one among our patrons. He was no fool, but rather very bright, intelligent, and well disposed, and when sober manifested many manly qualities. He was a genuine wit. One warm summer day, he came into the village on horseback, and rode up to the store. His horse, under the sting of flies and bees, became very restless, and in his efforts to fight the annoying insects, he kicked his hind foot into the stirrup with the foot of the rider. " Well, well," said R., addressing himself to the horse, " old fellow, if you are

Schoolmaster Becomes a Preceptor

going to get on, I must get off." Later on a very corpulent man in the neighborhood, weighing at least three hundred pounds, was taken sick and died. Mr. R. attended the funeral, and stood by the roadside, with other neighbors, when the funeral procession was passing. Turning to the person nearest to him, he whispered, "Really I should prefer, in this case, to be a *mourner* rather than a *bearer*."

NORTH GRANVILLE LADIES' SEMINARY

In the summer of 1855, having accepted the principalship of North Granville (N. Y.) Ladies' Seminary, we left Thetford, on many accounts regretfully, to enter upon the duties of this new position. A new school building, which would accommodate the family of the principal and some fifty boarding pupils, had been nearly completed, and a new school, in a new locality, was now to be gathered, mainly through my efforts. We were cordially welcomed by the citizens of the delightful village and the trustees of the seminary, and all seemed much interested in the enterprise which had been undertaken; but I soon found that the circumstances of the situation were peculiar. Instead of half a dozen schoolmen, wisely chosen on account of their fitness to manage a literary institution, I found a board of sixteen stockholders, who gained their positions as trustees by virtue of their investment, and they had formed this corporation and erected this seminary as a business speculation. They were reputable men of means, good citizens, and well disposed towards the principals and the school, but a majority of them were profoundly ignorant of their own rights and duties growing out of their relations as trustees to the principal whom they had elected to manage their seminary, and of his duties and obligations to the patrons and pupils of the school. Some results of this ignorance will appear in the course of my narrative.

The school opened very hopefully, early in September, and the prospect was entirely satisfactory to all interested. Fresh accessions of boarders came in at the opening of each new term, until the rooms were all filled. Fully understanding the situation, I was very careful to explain to the trustees my method of management and the school regulations I proposed to adopt, and secured their entire approval. But I soon found that some of these trustees, notwithstanding their approval of what I had proposed to do, and was doing, had expressed dissatisfaction, because at our evening receptions the young men of the town and neighboring towns were not freely admitted and introduced to our young ladies in the parlor. They would not object to the rule on this point as applied to the general public, but thought the stockholders had a right to invite and introduce whom *they* pleased. They had met and passed a vote to this effect, and sent a committee to me to ask my approval of this amendment to my laws. I requested a hearing before the board, which was granted. I reminded them that they had elected me to manage the school, and had approved my regulations, as explained to them, upon this very point. I said to them that the proposed change would offend the parents of our young ladies, and might prove a great injury to the school. Finally, I suggested that the school could not prosper under the management of seventeen heads, and if they had found that their principal was not capable of governing the school, I was ready to resign in favor of the man who could govern it, but I could not allow the trustees the favor they asked. The board was divided on the question of yielding the point. I left them to settle the matter in their own time and way. At the end of two weeks, I was informed that the members loyal to me had gained the victory, and that the board had passed a resolution, strongly expressed, giving me unbounded control. This put an end to all controversy as to the government of the school, and left me not only with the power, but also the responsibility of its management.

Another incident occurred during the second or third year at North Granville which excited much interest at the time, and is worthy of notice here. I had in my employment a teacher who had proved irresponsible both financially and morally. This teacher purchased a valuable piano of Oliver Ditson and Company of Boston, on trust (using my name without authority, to sustain his credit), promising to pay by instalments; but he had failed to make any payments, as agreed. He then mortgaged this instrument as security for a fifty-dollar debt due one of our trustees. I felt bound to notify Mr. Ditson, and in reply he sent me a receipted bill for the piano, and charged it to my account, directing me to hold the instrument at all hazards. The trustee who held the mortgage sent the sheriff to attach the instrument. I protested. The officer finally said to me, if I would give him my check for fifty dollars, as proof of my sincerity and pledge to meet him in court, to settle the ownership of the piano, he would not insist upon its removal. I did so, not suspecting that the officer was a rascal, as he proved to be. But instead of holding the check as he promised, as a pledge of good faith, he at once gave it to the trustee to whom the teacher owed fifty dollars, in payment of the debt. The check was drawn on my bank at Salem, twenty miles away. As soon as I learned the facts in the case, I sent a messenger to stop payment. The trustee sent another messenger to collect it, but my messenger reached the bank first, and payment was refused. I then told my friend, the trustee, that if he undertook to collect the amount on that check he would regret it afterwards. He finally gave me the check, but still determined to secure the piano which was in the seminary.

A lawyer in the neighborhood, who was one of my patrons, came to the rescue. He proposed to take the case in hand and get possession of the piano, relying for his fee upon what he could get out of the sale of the instrument above the fifty dollars due the trustee. On these terms he was employed as prosecuting counsel.

It was vacation at the seminary, and one morning the lawyer patron called at my office and paid my bill for the tuition of his daughter, and then said to me, " I am instructed to take possession of a piano belonging to your teacher, which is in the seminary." I replied, " My teacher does not own any piano in the seminary." " I know better," he answered, and started for the room where the piano was placed. I stepped in ahead of him and locked the door. He broke it open and placed an attachment upon the piano, and told me he would soon return with help to remove it. But when he came, he found a strong force of men in the room, who disputed his right to remove the piano. The struggle lasted all day, and at night the lawyer's party acknowledged defeat and retired.

At this point I ordered *this* piano to be sent that night to Salem depot, and shipped to Boston, and the next morning I sent a *rented* piano to our depot, belonging also to Oliver Ditson and Company, believing that the prosecuting lawyer would see it pass his house and go for it, with the impression that this was the identical instrument claimed under the mortgage. The strategy was effective, and a large force was sent to capture the prize. We met them with a show of force, to defend the property, but intentionally allowed them to triumph. They took the old piano from the depot under protest, and drove up through the village shouting triumphantly over their supposed victory, but when they landed it at the house of the trustee, they discovered that they had unlawfully taken a piano admitted to belong to another party, and carried it back to the depot, where it remained six months.

I at once sued, and put the case into the Supreme Court. The whole county was in commotion over the affair. This struggle between the preceptor of the seminary and the pettifogger had been announced in the papers, and the result was known to the lawyers at the court then in session, and my unfortunate lawyer patron fared hard under criticism. At the end of six months, he came and begged for a settlement, which I accepted on condition of payment by him of one hundred and fifty dollars cost and damage.

Thus peace was restored, the trustee smiled upon me submissively, and my

Schoolmaster Becomes a Preceptor

patron returned his daughter to my school. Mr. Oliver Ditson was greatly amused by the whole transaction, and proposed to publish a piece of music entitled " The Squabble Galop," dedicated to Lawyer Spencer; but he did not live to carry out his purpose.

Still another incident which occurred while I was in charge of North Granville Ladies' Seminary is fresh in memory. Its recital will lead to the discussion of an important and practical school question. Dr. Joseph E. King, then a young man, who had been my rival in Vermont, as principal of Newbury Academy, twenty miles from Thetford, went to New York State before I did, to take charge of Fort Edward Seminary, — a very large, mixed boarding-school. My school at North Granville, forty miles away, was exclusively for young ladies. Soon after I had opened my school, Principal King unmasked his battery, and gave me and my system a broadside through the public press. " Where shall we educate our daughters ? " was the question which he

119

undertook to answer, in a full-page article, in a large-sized weekly paper. Of course his conclusion was, that all parents should send their daughters to Fort Edward, to his model seminary, and not to North Granville to come under the " exclusive and aristocratic system of education" adopted there. His main argument, I remember, was based on the " Heaven-ordained family," in which our wise Creator purposed to educate together the brothers and sisters. He insisted that the school, which is an expansion of the family, should be modelled after the same plan. I at once answered the article, and caused the publication in every newspaper in the county.

To his main argument, I replied that there is a wide difference between the home with a half dozen children, of different ages, under the watchful care of anxious parents, and a boarding-school like Fort Edward, having from eight hundred to a thousand students of mature age, gathered from the cities, including, doubtless, many whose character would not bear investigation. In his rejoinder he took up my plea of moral danger, and insisted that it had no force, as applied to Fort Edward Seminary, because he had made ample provision to guard against this danger. His students, he assured his readers, occupied distinct departments, one for the girls and the other for the boys, and they were separated by a brick wall, with no entrance doors, and, on the outside, during the hours of darkness, an ample police force was employed to guard the premises. In my rejoinder, I commended his vigilance and painstaking, but ridiculed his *model family*; the idea of an old farmhouse with a brick wall running through the middle, and a policeman on the outside during the night, to keep the brothers and sisters apart !

The discussion continued six months, with increasing interest in the community; and the result, as affecting my interest, was a large increase of attendance at my school; and the climax of the discussion was an object lesson published in the same papers that had printed our articles, revealing the fact that one of Fort Edward's teachers

had been expelled for an offence growing out of the peculiar relations of this
monstrous family. Years afterwards, Dr.
King's school building was burned to the
ground, and in its place, under his direction, there was erected a fine school building, exclusively for young women, and Dr.
King, the able and venerable principal, is
still in charge (1898). That this discussion was not personal, the following
friendly note, recently received from the
genial Doctor, will show : —

FORT EDWARD, N. Y., July 6, 1897.

MY DEAR DR. ORCUTT, — From the height
of my lofty pyramid of friends, I reach *you* my
hand in greeting and congratulations. It is inspiring now and then to see a Nestor still fighting
in the front ranks. Your splendid persistence is
a powerful object.lesson to the coming generation. In good health and with a strong heart, I
am,

Most truly yours,

JOSEPH E. KING.

The question here naturally arises which
of these two systems, the mixed or the
separate school, should prevail ? With my

Schoolmaster Becomes a Preceptor

fifteen years' experience in managing mixed schools, and twenty-five years at the head of ladies' seminaries, I have formed a decided opinion on the subject, which I may here properly express. My decision is that in schools of the primary grade, — indeed in all public schools whose pupils come from their homes, or board with friends, — there is not only no objection to co-education, but much in its favor. In academies, where students find homes in good families, and the school is under efficient management, experience and observation confirm the opinion that the advantages and disadvantages nearly balance each other. In the boarding academy or seminary, especially where large numbers of students of mature age are associated, the mixed system is decidedly objectionable. In the college, as a rule, the mixed system is still more objectionable. When young women living near a college, and wishing to pursue that regular collegiate course of study, make application, there is no objection to admitting them. But the absolute union of the college for young

123

women with the college for young men would prove a serious disadvantage to both classes. To unite Wellesley with Williams, Smith with Dartmouth, or Vassar with Cornell, would be objectionable on the score of expense. As buildings could not be removed, the cost of the outfit would be at least double, and the expense of instruction would not be diminished. While it is admitted, yea claimed, that young women are quite equal to the young men they would meet in the classes, in scholarly ability, and would compete with them successfully for college honors, yet the education of the young woman for her sphere of life requires, to some extent, a different course of studies; and this fact adds much to the objections to college co-education. At our colleges established exclusively for women, the course of studies is adapted to their wants; and at our colleges established exclusively for young men, the course is suited to the training they need to fit them for their life work. To unite them would jeopardize the interest of both parties, resulting in no additional benefit to either; and it

will never be done. The discussion of
the main question will be continued, but
the union of these colleges will not be the
result. There are now four hundred and
fifty-one colleges and universities in this
country, and one hundred and forty-three
schools of higher learning, having thirty
thousand students, open to women *only*.
Forty-one colleges are absolutely closed to
women. These may, ere long, admit a few
women, as a matter of accommodation, as
others have done ; but will men ever be admitted into the colleges established for
women only? One hundred and forty-three
institutions are closed to men, against forty-
one closed to women. I have not here
discussed the moral side of the question,
but there is, as I have intimated, moral
danger in co-education, as arranged in
some large boarding-schools.

While *en route* from Thetford to North
Granville my dear wife, who had shared
with me the labors and trials of my
academic life, so far, expressed the fear that
I had made a mistake in giving up my
position where I had young men in train-

ing for college and for professional life, for one exclusively devoted to the education of young women. I replied that I thought that I had made no mistake, as the mothers and teachers of to-day will be the educators of the next generation of men and women, and so on through all time. I remembered the struggles of Mrs. Mary Hart Willard, in her girlhood, to secure an education for herself, and her heroic and successful efforts, in mature life, to establish and maintain a ladies' seminary at Troy, New York. She was the pioneer in this noble work. I recalled the marvellous struggle of Miss Mary Lyon, who, after serving an apprenticeship as an assistant in Mrs Grant's School for girls, in Ipswich, Massachusetts, opened " Mount Holyoke Female Seminary," and maintained there a school of high order to the day of her death ; that that seminary has grown into a first class college, and that under its inspiring influence Vassar, Wellesley, and Smith Colleges have sprung up, all laboring earnestly for the higher education of woman. I realized that the managers of these institutions have hold of the lever that moves the world ; and I was willing to contribute my share of effort and influence for the advancement of this noble course. I have never regretted that the last twenty-five years of my school life as preceptor were spent at the head of seminaries devoted exclusively to the education of young women.

The course of studies adopted at this school for graduation, as at my other schools, was broad and thorough. I made provision for the study of the ornamental branches, such as music, drawing, and painting, but insisted that they were only of secondary importance, and that the solid and disciplinary studies alone could lay the foundation for genuine scholarship and practical ability. I realized that only solid substances will take an ornamental polish. I have spent many hours in attempting to convince foolish mothers and would-be-lazy school-girls that a mere smattering or even a thorough knowledge of the ornamental branches, without the solid, and with a limited knowledge of common English branches, with no ability to write a respectable letter, is not an education. A full course of mathematics, including trigonometry, the classics, and literature, with one or more of the modern languages, the natural sciences, mental and moral philosophy, and a thorough course of history and English literature, are as important for young women as for young men.

Four large classes graduated from North Granville Ladies' Seminary during the five years of my administration. These graduates have made a good record as wives and teachers, and some of them have gained high distinction. Most of the teachers employed in this, as well as in my other seminaries, were educated in my schools. They ranked high, and were very successful. I recall three of special ability to handle classes: Miss Lucy Brown, as a teacher of mathematics, was a fine scholar and "apt to teach," in a remarkable degree. She died too early, if judged from a human point of view. Mrs. Eliza (Du Bois) Frost, in English branches, who is the widow of the lamented Prof. C. P. Frost, for many

years at the head of the Medical College
at Dartmouth. Her two sons are now
professors in Dartmouth College. Mrs.
Mary (Cobb) Hayes, for nine years a
prominent teacher in my seminary, and
since, for more than twenty years, the
principal of the best family boarding and
day school in the city of Boston. She
graduated from North Granville Ladies'
Seminary.

My engagement under this contract had
expired, and we had decided to seek a new
field of labor, though earnestly urged by
the trustees to renew the contract and remain. Professor Charles F. Dowd, the
originator of the change of time, as now
indicated in the East and West, and at
present and for many years principal of
Temple Grove Ladies' Seminary at Sara-
toga Springs, New York, was elected
principal in my place.

GLENWOOD LADIES' SEMINARY

IN July of 1860, we removed to West
Brattleboro, Vermont, to make ready to
open a ladies' seminary as a private

enterprise. I had leased the old Brattleboro Academy, with a boarding hall connected, and erected a new hall, having the
capacity for some sixty more boarders.
One hundred boarders could now be well
accommodated with rooms in both halls, and
at our long tables. I had furnished both of
these halls, and graded the grounds tastefully, building in the centre of a beautiful
lawn a fountain which was constantly throw-
ing into the air pure spring water from
the hillside. I had expended in the entire
outfit some twenty thousand dollars, and
had named the institution Glenwood Ladies'
Seminary,—a name suggested by the charm-
ing scenery by which it was surrounded.

I now selected my board of trustees and
visitors, such men as were sure to help, and
not trouble me. I sent out my circulars
announcing a full board of teachers for
every department of school work, and
advertised through the press the new enter-
terprise. I employed a new method of
free advertising not on the program of
advertising agencies.

A Brattleboro editor had taken great

pains to describe and extol this new enterprise in the town, and, in alluding to the
fountain on the lawn, he declared that it
would throw water sixty feet high! A
Burlington (Vermont) editor was very
sceptical, and forcibly expressed his dis-
belief in the statement; but the Brattleboro
quill-man insisted, and challenged investigation. This discussion lasted for several
weeks, during which all the prominent attractive features and advantages of the new
school were laid before the public. All
these sources of information, with the sound
of the hammer upon the new seminary
hall, had given Glenwood Ladies' Seminary
great notoriety, and the citizens of the whole
town were waiting with impatient interest
to witness the result. Some were hopeful
that we should not be disappointed, and
others very sceptical. Judge Clarke, one
of the oldest citizens of the town, and a
trustee of Brattleboro Academy, which I
had leased, reminded me one day that they
had for many years furnished the old
academy and quite a large boarding hall,
but it had never been half filled. He did

not understand, he said, why I had spent six thousand dollars in erecting a new hall before I knew that the old one would not fully accommodate all my boarding pupils. I asked him to wait, and I would show him reasons for my action.

September came, and the day appointed for opening the school. I went to the village depot to meet any students and teachers who might come on the evening train. On inquiry, I was told that the train was late, and that a telegram had announced the reason, viz.: "Three carloads of young women were at Bellows Falls on their way to Glenwood Seminary."

Before the end of that week, every available room in both halls was occupied, and twelve boarders had taken rooms in a neighboring cottage. Counting the day-students, one hundred and twenty-five young ladies and twelve teachers were in their places, and the school was organized and ready for work.

I had re-engaged several of the North Granville teachers, and some forty young ladies from that school had followed them

Schoolmaster Becomes a Preceptor

to Glenwood. Before the end of the first year Glenwood Ladies' Seminary was as well known throughout the country as many older schools, and the young ladies, returning home for vacations, were sure to bring back with them as many new students as necessary to fill the vacancies caused by the retiring of individuals and the graduating of classes. All that was now necessary, in providing for the future, was to make sure that a good school was maintained, and proper care taken of the business management.

At North Granville Seminary, I had given all the attention that could be given, without a gymnasium, to physical culture. The best substitute for the marching drill was the family dance in the public parlor, which was thoroughly enjoyed, and of great practical benefit. At Glenwood this long neglected and important branch of education was made prominent. A fine hall for the practice of gymnastics was ready for use, and the daily exercise was required of all the boarders. Every intelligent educator in the nation has always known that a sound body is a necessary condition of a sound mind, yet I am not aware that systematic physical culture was introduced into any school, private or public, in New York, Vermont, or New Hampshire, until I introduced it into my schools in these States.

This exercise is properly called gymnastics, and the term is equally applicable when applied to the development of mind or the body. To the body, it gives health, gracefulness, ease and steadiness of carriage, strength, elasticity, and quickness of movement, self-control, and endurance. To the mind, it imparts a healthful vigor to every faculty, as it is developed through exercise in the process of educational training. These facts are now everywhere recognized by intelligent educators.

For eight years, a large class of young ladies, having completed the prescribed course of study, graduated each year from Glenwood, and passed out into the busy world to engage in their life-work. During the fifth year, an earnest call came to me from the trustees of Tilden Ladies'

Seminary, at West Lebanon, New Hampshire, to accept the principalship of that institution. I declined to consider it, on the ground that I had already a large and prosperous school on my hands. The call was soon repeated, with the offer that I might retain my school at Glenwood, and conduct Tilden in my own way, with perfect freedom. I reconsidered my decision, and in view of the overflow of students at Glenwood, and some other circumstances, I decided to accept the position.

TILDEN LADIES' SEMINARY

TILDEN Seminary had been in operation ten years, under the management of three principals, the last of whom had made so complete a failure that not one student was left in the school to tell the tale of the disaster. The building, delightfully located on an estate of four acres, on the New Hampshire side of the Connecticut River, was erected mainly through the munificence of Mr. William Tilden of New York, as a memorial to his birthplace. It contained a pleasant parlor and schoolroom, and would accommodate the family of the principal and some fifty boarding pupils. I took a lease of the property, and proceeded to make the necessary arrangements to open the school in the spring of 1865, in connection with Glenwood, already well established.

As I have intimated, my family had been broken up. A new life had opened up before me, and I decided to make Tilden my future home, taking with me, as my wife, Miss Ellen L. Dana of Poughkeepsie, New York, who had been one of my teachers at Glenwood. It would not be possible to express in words the fidelity and loyalty with which she performed the duties of the responsible position which she assumed at Tilden, as preceptress, nor how large a part she has played as a beloved helpmeet and companion in whatever success I may have attained.

Putting the building in order, I issued circulars announcing a board of ten instructors, making complete provision for every department of a full and well-organized school, though no school was yet assured.

In April, the school opened with some seventy-five students, including the day scholars, and ere long all the rooms were occupied by boarders. I had now the charge of two ladies' seminaries, in two States, and seventy miles apart, with twenty associate and assistant teachers, and about two hundred lady students; and I divided my time between the two institutions, as circumstances required.

Mr. Tilden, the founder of the seminary which bears his name, attended the first commencement, and, becoming interested in the manifestly improved condition and prospects of the school, and realizing the need of more and better accommodations, decided to appropriate twenty thousand dollars to add two spacious wings to the building. These wings were finished, furnished, and equipped for use in process of time. A steeple and bell had already been placed upon the old building, and some two hundred evergreens, transplanted from the nursery, ornamented the grounds. Three thousand dollars had been contributed by the Tilden family to replenish the library and laboratory. Four years of the school's life under the present administration had now nearly expired, and the day was appointed for the annual commencement and dedication of the new building.

COMMENCEMENT AND DEDICATION

THIS was an occasion of great interest to the friends of Tilden Seminary. The exercises opened Sabbath morning, July 12, 1869, in the village church, with the baccalaureate sermon to the graduating class, by Rev. William S. Palmer, D.D., a former pupil of the principal while at Thetford Academy. His text was, "That our daughters may be as corner-stones polished after the similitude of a palace," a passage of Scripture which had been used as a motto in our catalogue. The graduating class numbered seventeen young ladies, representing eight different States. The examinations covered three full days, and received marked attention. The gymnastic exercise in the new gymnasium, conducted by my daughter, Miss Mary F. Orcutt, the teacher in that department for six years, was attended by more than four hundred spectators. The dedicatory exercise in the church was fully attended by an appreciative audience. The church was tastefully ornamented with evergreen. Over the front of the stage was suspended the class motto, *Finis Coronat Opus.* At the rear of the platform was placed a pedestal on which stood the bust of Mr. Tilden, draped in black, with vases of white flowers on either side. Above this was suspended the inscription in large letters, " Our Lamented Benefactor." This motto was an expression of the feeling of sadness and regret felt by the audience that Mr. Tilden could not have been spared to witness this crowning glory of his benevolent enterprise.

Colonel J. D. Hosley, one of the trustees, and chairman of the building committee, made an address and delivered the new charter and keys to Mr. William Tilden Blodgett, a nephew of the founder, and his representative on this occasion. Mr. Blodgett made an interesting address in transferring the charter and keys to President Smith of Dartmouth College, who represented the trustees. Dr. Smith responded in an appropriate and eloquent address. The singing of an original dedication hymn closed these exercises. A large audience gathered in the church in the evening to listen to an address by President James B. Angell, LL.D. (recently appointed by President McKinley as minister to Turkey), the reading of the report by the chairman of the examining committee, Rev. C. C. Parker, of Gorham, Maine, and the address of the principal in conferring the diplomas upon the graduating class. The singing of the class hymn, composed by one of its members, closed the exercises of the week and day.

This triumphant commencement, revealing as it did the great improvements which had been made in the seminary, and the increased facilities now offered, attracted public attention, and ere long the wings as well as the body of the new seminary were filled with boarders. The new gymnasium gave opportunity for perfecting the arrangements for systematic physical culture, and it was improved. This new department of instruction attracted special attention. In course of the three years that the principal was a member of the General Court, from Lebanon, a large delegation from that body, on their way to Dartmouth College, called at Tilden to witness the gymnastic drill of the young ladies, and expressed great satisfaction.

My early adoption and extensive use of Dr. Dio Lewis's system of gymnastics led to a personal acquaintance with its author. He was the originator of this system, and an enthusiast upon the subject, and he infused his own spirit into all with whom he came in contact. The subject was then new, and attracted much public interest and the usual amount of criticism from bigoted conservatives which every new departure from old methods is doomed to meet. All-wise fathers and conceited educators told us that their boys and girls had enough of physical exercise on the farm, in the work-shop, and at their homes, and needed no more; that their time in school should be devoted to study, and that already too many subjects were introduced into the schoolroom. Horrified mothers cried out in alarm against the indelicacy and impropriety of the gymnastic suit required for their daughters in practice. The townspeople nicknamed this exercise the " Orthodox dancing school." Still Dr. Lewis persisted in the necessity of systematic physical development of the human body, by such a drill as his system required, for health and vigor. Schools for instructing teachers to teach gymnastics were established. Harvard and Yale and Amherst and Dartmouth soon employed gymnastic teachers, and required regular gymnastic exercises. The subject was discussed at our educational meetings and, ere long, all the better academies and seminaries in the land introduced physical culture as a regular school exercise. Modified systems have been introduced, and, to-day, no branch of education is more popular or more in demand than gymnastics for every grade of school, from the kindergarten to the college. Many features of Dr. Dio Lewis's system yet hold the public favor, and are retained in practice.

The beneficial influence of this exercise

upon the health of students was demonstrated and recognized during the few years
of our Tilden school life. Professor Phelps,
then at the head of the medical department
of Dartmouth College, came to Tilden to
visit his daughter and niece, then in the
school. During an interview with the
principal, he very properly took occasion
to suggest the great danger to which the
young ladies were exposed, with no motive
or opportunity for physical activity, and
proceeded to prescribe a course of treatment to prevent the inevitable evil results.
The young ladies should not be required
to study too many hours, should be regular
in their habits of eating and sleeping, and
should have at least three hours' exercise
daily in the open air. I listened to him
with attention and interest, and replied that
I fully appreciated the wisdom and importance of his suggestions and instructions,
and that I had given much attention to the
health of my two large families at Tilden
and Glenwood. In addition to insisting
upon regularity of habits and free exercise
in the open air, I required a daily, sys-

tematic drill in gymnastics, and, to show him the results of my treatment, I told him that during one year of school-life experience with these two families, numbering at least one hundred and fifty boarders, the services of a physician had not been required in a single instance. He seemed greatly surprised and interested, and said evidently I did not need his advice or prescriptions.

This duplicate school arrangement, in managing Glenwood and Tilden Seminaries, lasted three years. At the end of this time, finding the care and labor excessive and somewhat burdensome, I sold out my interest at Glenwood, but continued my school at Tilden for twelve years, making fifteen years from the time I began here, with continued prosperity. One thousand young ladies had been enrolled at Tilden, and fifteen classes had graduated.

Thirty-eight years had now elapsed since I commenced my academic life. During this time, from Thetford, North Granville, Glenwood, and Tilden, six hundred and four had graduated. Of these one hundred and forty-seven were young men, and four hundred and fifty-seven young women. Nearly all the young men completed a collegiate course of study. A very large proportion of the women, after teaching a while, were married, and many others have occupied important positions in the school and in the family. The summary enrolment in all my public and private schools, during these forty years, was more than five thousand.

While still connected with Tilden Seminary, its twenty-fifth anniversary was celebrated, with great interest and enthusiasm, by a large gathering of former students, teachers, and other friends of the institution. The principal delivered the address of welcome, which was followed by addresses of great interest, delivered by Hon. Richard B. Kimball, LL.D., the distinguished author, and the late ex-Senator J. W. Patterson of New Hampshire.

Two facts may properly be mentioned here in regard to the academic institutions over which I presided. First, not one of them was endowed, they were all either new schools, or in a low condition in consequence of neglect or unskilful management.

Secondly, a very large majority of the students attending these schools were in moderate circumstances, and many were absolutely unable to prosecute their studies without aid. Scores of the latter class came to me for help ; and I adopted the rule never to reject an applicant of approved character, ability, and promise on account of poverty. Some needed only partial assistance ; others I carried through, providing board and tuition, and sometimes books and stationery also, entirely on trust. Such bills in the aggregate amounted to thousands of dollars. Many of those who contracted such debts made payment in full years afterwards ; others failed to do so for reasons beyond their control ; and a very few proved false and unworthy of the confidence I had placed in them. My experience in dealing with this class of students led me to believe that young women who have the ambition, ability, and energy to prosecute, with success, a course of study, but have not the ready money to pay expenses, are quite as reliable and worthy of trust as young men in similar circumstances.

VI

VITAL EDUCATIONAL QUESTIONS

DURING my long experience as a teacher, many young men and women have asked my advice and opinion on various subjects which have a direct bearing on educational training. I therefore digress for the time from the autobiographical narrative, hoping that these suggestions will be of value to those following in my footsteps, as they are the result of a long tuition under that sternest of masters, " experience."

ELEMENTS OF SUCCESS IN SCHOOL LIFE

I MAY here inquire what are the elements necessary for the success of the pupil and student, of the schoolmaster and of the preceptor, in their several spheres of action? The success of the scholar depends not so much upon what others do for him as upon what he does for himself; not so much upon favorable opportunities and increased facilities, as upon the proper use of such as he already enjoys. A good school, with skilful teachers and a large library, are useful and important; but they have no power to impart scholarship and to create manhood and womanhood.

The mental athlete is the product of mental gymnastics. The ability to think, reason, and debate is acquired only by thinking, reasoning, and debating. Knowledge is not the chief aim or end of study, but mental discipline and culture. To solve a hard problem or to translate a difficult Latin or Greek sentence, is valuable mainly as a mental victory; and often a failure to learn or recite a lesson is of more value to the student than success, as it may have cost him a greater effort. He who has gained the mastery over his own mental faculties, and the power of fixed attention and continued study upon the subject under investigation, is educated; and the only condition of such an attainment is hard and persistent application.

The success of the schoolmaster depends upon common sense, skill, and an
earnest devotion to the work in hand. I
have made a distinction in this treatise
between the schoolmaster and the preceptor; have confined the schoolmaster to
the public school, large or small, as the
case may be, in which he has to teach and
govern a promiscuous group of children
and youth of different ages, dispositions,
and conditions in life, and at the same
time deal with a whole neighborhood of
fathers and mothers, uncles and aunts,
grandfathers and grandmothers, some of
whom are likely to claim the right to
advise and dictate and criticise at every
point of his experience. Common sense,
which is the most uncommon of all human
endowments, is indispensable for such a
task. This alone will enable him to adapt
himself to circumstances, and always to say
and do the right thing at the proper time
and in the best manner. The teacher who
is destitute of this attribute is like a ship
without an anchor. He may sail on successfully in fair weather, but when the

storm rages he is at the mercy of the waves.

Both common sense and skill are natural gifts, and the candidate who is destitute of one or both had better seek some other employment than school-keeping. Earnest devotion to his work is another prerequisite to success. The schoolmaster should understand that his school duties should occupy all his time and thought, and engage all his strength and energy. The man or woman who keeps school with a divided interest has no right to undertake a work so important.

The preceptor holds a different position in some respects, hence he must possess some additonal qualifications. He is required not only to keep school and deal with his patrons, but in many of our academies and seminaries he has to create his school, each term and year of his administration. These institutions depend upon public patronage for a supply of students, and must rely upon the popularity and personal efforts of the principal. Hence he must possess not only ability to teach and govern, but the power to win public favor and draw in students from towns near and far away, over a large territory, and to contend with persistent competition. His school must gain public favor through his own personality and wise activity. If he cannot attract public attention and gain public favor, he will fail, though he may be an able teacher and disciplinarian. The power to will and hold public favor is also a natural gift, and must be possessed in addition to the other qualifications of the schoolmaster as described above. After all, the most important word in the teacher's vocabulary is *enthusiasm*. From the gleanings of my school-life experience, I here offer the young teacher the following : —

Pedagogic Truths and Suggestions

"The teacher is born and not made," but the "born teacher" must be educated.

"As the teacher is, so is the school."

The school is an expansion of the family, and the teacher acts *in loco parentis*.

That the teacher should be a *noble* man or woman is of great importance.

Every teacher should be professionally educated, and should improve every opportunity for self-culture while in service.

All digested knowledge is helpful to the teacher.

The teacher must enjoy the schoolroom, to be successful in it.

The physiology and psychology of the educational problem are absolutely essential.

The teacher needs a courage that never fails, and a faith that never falters.

The teacher should never fret nor scold in the presence of his pupils.

A skilful teacher is more important for the school than approved methods.

The good teacher is a character-builder.

Example is more effective than teaching.

The teacher's success or failure is usually settled the first week of school.

The wise teacher encourages self-respect and self-reliance in his pupils.

Discipline is a means and not an end; it is a stimulant as well as a restraint.

Love of thinking and skill of thought work wonders.

Industry is the best remedy for disorder in the schoolroom.

Ridicule and sarcasm should never be indulged in the school.

A noisy teacher makes a noisy school.

The eye is more potent than the voice in preserving order.

Education is neither a process of "pouring in" nor of "drawing out," but of "training up."

Pupils are sharp critics of their teachers, and good judges of their merits.

The school is making the future citizens of our Republic good or bad.

The patriotic teacher alone is qualified to train our children for citizenship.

Women teachers are coming to the front, and are a great power in our nation.

Enthusiasm in the teacher works wonders.

Self-control is the teacher's great security.

Independent thinking is an end to be sought in school-work.

Sympathy is an essential element in the teacher's life.

All teaching should be practical.

To lead and feed the mind of pupils is the important mission of the teacher.

Study the peculiarities and limitations of your pupils.

Teach subjects and not books.

Read professional books and papers.

Make free use of a note-book.

Do your part toward making teaching a profession.

Don't quarrel with your school-board.

Visit parents at their homes, form an intimate acquaintance with them, and invite them to visit your school.

Keep politics out of school.

Be willing to be advised, but unwilling to be controlled.

Make your school as pleasant and attractive as possible.

Encourage manly and ladylike behavior at all times and everywhere.

Teach your pupils how to use books, and how to study.

Celebrate and draw lessons from national holidays.

Vital Educational Questions

Draw lessons from the field, forest, and garden, and from the starry heavens.

Wake up the minds of your pupils.

Do nothing for the pupil that he can do for himself.

Encourage pupils by praise where praise is due.

Teach promptness and punctuality by example as well as by precept.

Call the attention of your pupils to buds, blossoms, and birds, and to the insect world.

Encourage the planting of trees around the schoolhouse ; they will live after you are gone.

Consider home life in dealing with school life.

Aim first of all to gain the confidence and affection of your pupils.

Discriminate between the act and the motive of your pupils.

Be both merciful and just.

Say *yes* and *no* with emphasis, but pleasantly.

Appeal to the pupil's nobility.

Never threaten punishment for an uncommitted act.

Teach morality and religious obligation.
Have faith in your pupils.

This last suggestion, like all the rest, is of great practical importance. In commenting on it, I wish to bring to view the skilful teacher at work, and quote an example or two to illustrate.

The teacher I have in mind wields a power whose strength is magical. She talks to her pupils as if she expected they desired to do right, and only needed to be shown how. She *does* expect it. The influence of her faith is felt by them, and they are elevated by it. If they fail, she expresses surprise and sorrow. A boy has carelessly written out his exercise. His teacher proposes to have him remain after school to copy it, not as an arbitrary and forced, but as a voluntary, punishment. She says to him: " I think you had better remain a few minutes to-night and copy this exercise. You probably did not realize how carelessly you had written it. This is not up to your best effort, and you will not be satisfied to have it stand as it is. Here is paper, pen and ink, and I know you will do this for

Vital Educational Questions

my sake and your own." With a blush of shame the boy seats himself for his voluntary task.

Another case in point: Jim, a heedless, reckless lad, commits an offence, and is called to account for it. Jim meets his confidential friend Jake, and tells him the story of his treatment, as follows. " Do yer know why I did n't lie out of it? Mebbe yer 'll think I was all-fired silly, but I jest could n't. My teacher called me up quiet-like and said: ' Now, Jim, I know your faults and I know your virtues. You ain't no coward, Jim, and yer won't lie even if yer should have ter take a licken. Some boys will say the square thing when they think they won't git licked, and some boys will tell the square thing anyway. A fellow like you, who could grab a little kid out from under a runaway horse like you did poor Sammy Smithers, ain't agoin' to be no coward now. Whatever yer tells me, Jim, I 'll believe, and there the thing ends, for I won't ask no one else !' Then I said, ' Why don't yer ask Willie Perkins, as he allus does what yer say?' But she said *she'd believe me as quick as any feller in the school.* Think of that, Jake! And then I jest up and told her, and she said she was awful sorry I done it, for the principal said he'd lick the boy, and course I'd have to git licked. I said 'course,' and I tuck the licken. Feel kind o' sore outside, but awful quiet-like inside. I'll do it again too. You bet she's right when she says, 'Jim, yer have yer faults but yer ain't no coward!' Most folks think I'm a tough; she don't. *She knows I won't lie,* and I won't lie never no more."

If the teacher would control and educate her pupils, build up their character, and fit them for the duties and responsibilities of life, she must have faith in them, and treat them accordingly.

THE COLLEGE OR THE UNIVERSITY— WHICH?

THE author has been asked hundreds of times by anxious parents whether he advised sending a boy to college or to a university, and the question is one which demands careful consideration.

Vital Educational Questions

The American college is the fountain-head of all the educational institutions and influence of the nation. The civilizing and elevating power of the college is felt through the academies, seminaries, public and private schools which are established on the hillsides and in the valleys, in every State of the Union. It is the source of them all.

Our fathers *first* planted the college, and *afterwards* the public free schools. The latter flowed from the former, as streams from a fountain. Elevating influences always descend from the higher to the lower, but never ascend from the lower to the higher. The profounder learning of the college gives tone and sentiment to the public mind, and nourishes and sustains popular education among the masses.

The college matures and develops the science which is learned in the elementary and higher schools, and educates, directly or indirectly, all the teachers and authors in every department of learning.

To illustrate: The ocean is the source of the water supply of the world. Without this fountain, we could have no rain, no springs, no rills, no rivulets, no rivers. These supply our wants directly; but all the water that falls from the clouds and fills the springs and flowing streams must come *first* from the ocean. We do not fill our pitcher from the sea, but all the water we dip from the spring comes from the sea. Dry up the fountain and the spring will disappear. So it is with the college. Close its doors, and ere long the academies and public schools would be closed. Instruction would cease, and finally civilization would give place to semi-barbarism.

The sun is the fountain and source of light. We might get on with twilight and moonlight; but blot out the sun from the heavens, and even these sources of dim light would be extinguished, and total darkness ensue. So with the college, which is the source of intellectual and moral light. Destroy this luminary, and the darkness of ignorance and superstition would, in time, cover the nation as a dreary mantle.

Still again, we are indebted to the college for all the influence that emanates from the learned professions. The college creates and sustains the profession of law, medicine, teaching, and the ministry.

The university differs from the college in its aim and scope. It may instruct students whom it afterwards examines for a degree, as in Germany and the United States ; it may do little or no teaching, but simply examine and confer degrees, as in England.

The University of Paris was the mother of universities, the precursor and exemplar of Oxford and Cambridge, as these institutions are of Harvard and Yale. The old Paris University disappeared in 1808, under the famous decree of Emperor Napoleon, leaving all the institutions of advanced learning in the nation under one name, — the University of France ; but the University of Paris was restored to its former prestige in 1896, under the auspices of the President of the French Republic. The inauguration was attended by a learned and illustrious audience. The addresses by the President of the University Council and the Minister of Public Instruction were worthy of the great occasion; they were full of enthusiasm, and of special interest to American educators.

These addresses, which President Gilman of Johns Hopkins University has made the theme of an able and instructive magazine article, reveal the function of the modern university. It is not merely an institution for imparting special kinds of knowledge for professional purposes, but also for advancing general knowledge and facilitating its acquirement by students whose aims are purely scientific.

The points made in these lectures illustrate the supreme advantages of the university. The result of uniting in one body all the chairs of superior instruction, with the introduction of their laboratories thirty years ago, was to make the institution thoroughly practical. The lectures, purely theoretical and mental, which were the method of imparting instruction in the old university, are only a memory in the new. The entire establishment is one immense factory, marvellous in its adaptation to the diversity of scientific work.

Vital Educational Questions

The concentration in the modern university of subjects most diverse is intentionally designed and adapted to give all its students opportunity to acquire that general knowledge which makes a truly cultivated man ready to enter upon the study of his profession or the duties of active life. In this course of study the dominant thought is " the unity of knowledge, the value of ascertained truth, and the importance of scientific methods of inquiry." The practical uses of knowledge are here emphasized.

It is of great interest to mark the marvellous improvements which have been made during the last fifty years in the process of evolution, in the oldest as well as in the youngest universities, in the old world as well as in the new. President Gilman, while he insists that American education is far behind European, that " American youth compared with those of foreign countries have lost two or three years of time," shows the progress which has been made in American institutions, and points out the remedies for our deficiencies.

First, these improvements are manifest from the institutional point of view. "During recent years," he says, "the Institutional has been considered more than the Industrial organization. Administration, finance, architecture, equipment have been the dominant themes. It is wonderful to survey the country from Bowdoin in the far northeast, with its gem of an art gallery, to Leland Stanford on the Pacific Coast, with its beautiful academic halls; from Minneapolis and Chicago in the upper Mississippi valley, to New Orleans and Austin (Texas), and observe that every strong institution is growing stronger and richer."

President Gilman claims that underlying all our deficiencies there is the want of organization and correlation. He says: "It is not likely that American education will be satisfactory to the most thoughtful people until it is far more systematic than at present, until the relations of all grades, from the kindergartens to the professional schools, are adjusted to one another by such a definite consensus as will be binding like a common law." He looks to the improvements that are in progress to correct this evil. He adds that, "A recent writer for a new German cyclopædia of education states that among nearly five hundred institutions in the United States which bear the name of college or university, there are nine entitled to rank with those of Europe." He thinks no careful American would have made this claim a generation ago. Mark here the fact that President Gilman regards the college and not the university as the disciplinary institution.

The distinction between the university and the college is one which must occur to every parent who has a son seeking for a collegiate education. We have already considered the theoretical features of each, — but how shall we put these theories into practical use in selecting a seat of learning for our son? In discussing this question, let us employ the word "university" in referring to such institutions as Harvard or Yale, and "college" in speaking of the smaller institutions, such as Dartmouth, Brown, Williams, or Amherst.

The university has a larger endowment than the college, a broader course of study, a larger, and in many cases an abler faculty, a more complete library, and a more extensive outfit in every department of instruction.

The university, because of its larger numbers, offers a superior opportunity to its students in that development which results from a daily contact with many other students of many varying characteristics. In the university our sons will see before them all " sorts and conditions of men," — some rich, some poor; some fast, some idle; some as noble specimens of manhood as the world can produce. Concerning each of these classes they must form their own conclusions, assimilating the best, avoiding the worst; and their success or their failure in doing this will determine their success or their failure in life. All this is true in the college, but it must be to a lesser degree. In short, our sons will gain a knowledge of manhood in the university which they could but partially gain in the college.

Vital Educational Questions

The university, because of larger numbers than in the college, contains a greater per cent of students whose friendships and associations we wish our sons to enjoy. These friendships have an immense bearing on the position which the students will occupy during their later life, and we owe it to them that they be given the best and widest opportunities in forming friendships. Further than this, the degree bestowed by the university will give its graduates a prestige which the college degree cannot give, and it is a parent's duty to give his son as perfect an equipment for his life-work as lies within his power.

There is still a third gain in the influence of the university course, — that of encouraging a thorough preliminary education for those who seek to enter the professions. It aims first to make men before it offers them to the professional schools, thus placing these institutions above the rank of trade schools.

On the other hand, the college fills a most honored position in the educational world. President Gilman, in the article to

which reference has already been made,
rejoices in "the recognition of an important
distinction between the disciplinary period
of liberal education commonly known in
this country as 'the college,' and the freer
opportunities of more advanced culture
which belong to the university." It is
here that the keynote of the college is
struck, — its greatest power is as a disciplinary institution.

In a following chapter we have discussed
the requirements of the preparatory school,
but unfortunately it is not possible for all
those who desire a collegiate education to
come under the discipline which these leading schools enforce. Circumstances are
often such that without the college higher
education must necessarily be abandoned.
There is absolute need of this individual
discipline at some educational period, and
unless this has been received in the preparatory school, it must be gained from the
college, — the university would not give
it. President Gilman urges the great need
of this personal instruction and influence.
He says that the experience of the world

has demonstrated that while there are magnificent and surprising exceptions to the rule, the average man is greatly helped by submission, during all his adolescence, to the precept, example, criticism, and suggestion of those who have, themselves, been well-trained. By such influences, character, physical, intellectual, and moral, is most likely to be harmoniously developed." It appears to him that "a liberal education would be much more highly valued, and would be much more advantageous to the world, if a greater amount of personal submission attended its progress." He quotes Ralph Waldo Emerson's criticism on this point. "Individuality, reads the sign-post," said Emerson ; "persons by themselves, not persons enrolled in classes. Our actual mode of procedure aims to do for masses what cannot be done for masses, what must be done reverently one by one."

The many opportunities now offered by the university to needy students to assist themselves, in addition to the liberal bestowal of scholarships, are well shown by the phamphlets issued by Harvard and Yale, and thus one of the greatest obstacles to a university education is removed. Undoubtedly the expense is greater, but the difference is at least equalled by the additional opportunities. It has practically been demonstrated that the mere fact that the student has not the available money in sight need not deter him from taking the course.

The immensity of the university, the apparent merging of individuality into the great mass of the student world, the additional temptations because of the lack of personal contact with the professors, and a thousand and one other doubts, tend to outbalance, in many cases, the manifest advantages. The parent, however, must not make the mistake of thinking that by restricting his son's environment he is preparing him to hold his own in the world, with which he is bound to come in contact only a few years later. The innate qualities of the boy will come to the surface sooner or latter, whether they be good or bad, and if the latter predominate, they will be quite as apparent in the college as in the university.

To sum up the question, I would say that it all depends upon the boy and the previous education he has been able to obtain. If he has lost the development to be gained by the individual and recitation work of an ample preparation, the college is the better place for him; if he has already had this experience, give him the greater opportunity for the all-around development which the university offers.

PREPARATION FOR COLLEGE AND LIFE

I. The Duty of the Home

IT is a natural question on whom the greatest responsibility falls in the preparation of pupils for college and for life. Let us glance first at the responsibility which falls upon the home.

The school and the college are an expansion of the family. The parent in the home is the Heaven-ordained disciplinarian of his children. The master in the school and the president in the college act under delegated authority, *in loco parentis*. Government in all these relations is based upon the same principle, modified in administration only by the varying circumstances of the situation. If all the families in the States were properly trained, we would have a right to infer that the children in the schools and the students in the academy, college, and university would be law-abiding and loyal to the authority under which they are placed. Hence when we meet with disorder and insubordination in the public schools, we naturally attribute the evil to laxity of family discipline. And when we hear of rioting and rebellion in the academy or college, as we so often do in these days, we say that the reckless and rebellious students were not properly governed in the home and in the school; and for the same reason we infer that the unsubdued children, pupils and students, are likely to become lawless citizens and candidates, in every community, for the prison and the gallows.

It cannot be denied that the spirit of lawlessness and insubordination prevails now more extensively and alarmingly in our public institutions than in the earlier period of our country's history; and it is equally true, that a great change has occurred in the theory and practice of family and school government. The discipline of our fathers and the teachers of their day was based upon authority; obedience to wholesome rules and regulations was demanded and enforced; but in many cases, in these days, persuasion is substituted for authority, and all power to control has been lost in family government. Hence when these children come into the school, the teacher, even if he is qualified and disposed to enforce unqualified obedience, is forbidden to do so by school officers, except by moral means.

Now the question is, — Is there any connection between these two facts, as cause and effect? May not this be the reason why some children become insubordinate pupils in the school, reckless students in the college, and lawless citizens in the community?

Professor Albion W. Small of the University of Chicago, in a recent discussion at the meeting of the National Educational Association at Milwaukee, Wisconsin, expressed forcibly his views upon this point. " I take square issue," he said, " upon the question of *enforcing* wholesome laws in our schools. It is a mistaken policy, adopted by our school authorities, to leave to pupils themselves to fix the standard of their own conduct; to allow them to decide that only to be right to which they consent, and that only to be positively binding upon them to which they agree. Many schools have surrendered to unwise parents who have previously capitulated to their children. The abolition of corporal punishment is an incident in this surrender. This is virtual treason against the sovereignty of law. They tell us that it cultivates self-respect and self-control in pupils when school authorities shirk the duty of requiring propriety of conduct on pain of effective penalties. This flimsy claim springs either from ignorance or stupid sympathy, or it is a part and parcel of the cringing subserviency which has made much of our self-government a stench at home and a byword abroad. The schools should make *patriots*, but by this policy they are doing much to make *anarchists*. This anarchism is inculcated by family and school government which stops short of compulsion in dealing with children before they have developed the habit of effective morality."

Dr. Lyman Abbott of Brooklyn, New York, in a lecture on Education before the same body, fully indorsed Professor Small's theory. He said: "In order to educate the people for self-government, there must be lodged somewhere in the public school the power to enforce law, and compel the lawless and recalcitrant to obey the law; for one who has not learned to obey the law has not learned to exercise government."

II. The Duty of the Preparatory School

THE endowed academy still survives, and will hold through all time an important place among our institutions of learning. The high school cannot, in all respects, fill the place of the academy, but it is rapidly approaching it in efficiency. As a fitting school for college, no other can equal this well-endowed, well-furnished, and professionally taught classical school. It does more than any other can do to awaken the mind, to inspire young men and women with lofty ambition, and to cultivate a taste for classical learning and for broad and extensive culture. It encourages social relations, the most favorable for securing the best results of a practical education. The modern academy is distinguished from the ancient only by the greater and better facilities it affords, and by its improved methods of instruction.

Upon the efficiency of these secondary schools depends the standing and success of the college and the university, and of the classes which graduate from these institutions in their life work. Both the academy and the college have manifestly made great progress during the last half century. They have become more thorough and more practical, and the better class have raised their standard of requirements for

admission and graduation; have extended
their curriculum, and increased their corps
of instructors.   It has been stated that
there are probably a hundred seats of learning in the United States, to-day, better
provided with material aids to education
than Harvard or Yale were fifty years ago.
But these universities still hold their advanced position, and are constantly demand-
ing of the preparatory schools, which are
their principal feeders, better and still better
preparation for entrance.   The leading colleges, such as Dartmouth, Brown, Amherst,
and Williams, have also raised their standard and require a corresponding advance in
the preparatory schools which supply them
with students.   For ten years, from 1790
to 1800, Dartmouth led Harvard, Yale, and
Princeton in the number of graduates, but
was unable to keep up successful competition for the want of funds and perhaps
other reasons.

Much excitement has recently been produced by the demand of Harvard upon her
preparatory schools for a better preparation of their graduates in the English

language. Some of the masters of these schools resented the charge that they had not given sufficient attention to the study of our language, which led to a spirited discussion through the press and in teachers' conventions. But the facts showing the deficiency in students who had entered the university demonstrated the justice and importance of the criticism. It is a hopeful indication that our educators are giving attention to this subject. There is no reason why the English language should not be studied with as much care and thoroughness as the classics or the modern languages. Indeed, it is reasonable to claim that for English students a complete and practical knowledge of "our mother tongue" should be regarded as of the first importance. It is a lamentable fact that many students and graduates of our colleges and universities are unable to speak and write the English language correctly and skilfully.

There is another point of great importance, especially to those who design to enter the university. The disciplinary period of a liberal education is an indispensable process in development. Study and recitation are the means by which all practical attainments are secured, and the recitation is, at least, as important as the study. Hence the class drill, during the disciplinary process, cannot be omitted without serious loss. The student should not only learn his lesson, but he should recite it under criticism.

All practical lessons in life are learned by recitation. The child learns to walk and talk by walking and talking; the mechanic learns to use his tools by using them; the musician learns to sing and play on the instrument; and the orator to sway his audience by constant and long-continued practice. The art of easy and graceful conversation and correct composition is acquired only by conversing and composing. All these are recitations. Thus no lesson is thoroughly learned until the thought contained therein has been intelligently expressed in recitation.

Now this disciplinary work belongs properly to the preparatory school, and if it is not secured there the student is not fitted to enter the university, to gain the finishing culture of a complete liberal education. Thus the modern preparatory school holds an important position in our educational system, and the college and the university have the right to expect and demand thorough preparatory work, and in this way only can they secure it.

THE MORAL SIDE OF SCHOOL LIFE

THE moral side of school life should be especially emphasized as an essential part of education. In my forty years' practice I have endeavored to make this thought prominent. In my books previously written, I have strongly urged its claims upon teachers and parents, and through all my school life the conviction has grown upon me that the chief end of all education is to produce men and women morally trained for their life work. Physical culture is essential, but this alone may only fit the man for a prize-fighter, and make him a brute in human form. "Intellectual culture without the moral," some one has said, "only prepares the madman for suicide;" while

the proper training of the *whole* man, physically, intellectually, and morally, gives him
strength, power, and integrity, with ability
to act well his part in whatever position in
life he is called to labor.

Scholarship is desirable as a result of
school training, but its attainment is in no
way hindered, but rather facilitated, by
proper attention to moral culture. The
true teacher is not only a scholar maker,
but also a character builder.

In reviewing his school life the author
has cumulative evidence of the correctness
of his theory and the importance of his
practice. The children and students under
his instruction fifty years ago are now fill-
ing, or have filled, important and responsible positions in active life : in the family
as parents, training another generation of
children for life's duties and for immortal-
ity ; in the school as teachers, shaping the
course and moulding the character of aspiring youth who are ere long to take their
places ; in the college, as presidents and
professors, guiding young men and women
who are to enter the learned professions ;

in every community all over the nation, as citizens of this great Republic, conducting the important affairs of State and Church, and discharging the duties of social life; in the professions, exerting a controlling influence in public affairs; in the halls of legislation, and on the bench of justice, making and administering laws that control seventy millions of people and affect the weal or woe of the nation.

Now what have given these thousands of men and women the power they have gained and exercised? I answer, the manly and womanly *character* which was formed under the moral influence and instruction exerted and given in the homes and schools of their childhood and youth. If any have failed, it was for the want of this important training.

The moral includes the religious but not the sectarian teaching in schools. It is not the parochial teaching of dogmatic theology, nor the careless reading of the Bible in our public schools, that is so much needed. It is, first of all, the influence of the living teacher whose life has been consecrated to

the service of God and mankind, whose
soul is aglow with enthusiasm, who is in
love with his work and feels the responsibility of his position.

The example of such a teacher has great
moral power over his pupils. It uncon-
sciously encourages the right and discour-
ages the wrong in their daily lives, and
moulds them into likeness. Such a teacher
has the moral wants of his pupils constantly
in view, and seeks and improves every
opportunity to impart moral lessons. Incidents occurring every day involve moral
principles. He seizes upon them as texts
for moral lessons, and enforces them by
the examples before him.

For instance, in dealing with school
vices, the teacher has detected a pupil in
falsehood. This is his opportunity to give
a practical lecture before the whole school
upon the cowardice, folly, and sin of lying.
Another pupil is suspected of stealing, but
it is not positive that he is the guilty party.
The master brings the matter before the
school, explains the nature and consequences of such an act upon the present

and future of the pupil's life, and suggests, if the boy has repented and made restitution, that he may not be reported to the school, but that the praiseworthiness of his repentence and confession may be commended and emphasized. Profane language has been overheard on the playground. The master now speaks to the school upon the low vulgarity of profanity. He is called upon to settle a quarrel in which the strong has abused the weaker party, and he gives the school a practical lesson on individual rights and the manliness of generosity and kindness. He reads in the newspaper an account of one who rescued a fellow-student from drowning, at the risk of his own life. Here is a text for an effective lesson on heroism. Washington's and Lincoln's birthdays occur, and are improved to impart lessons of patriotism. Thousands of cases like these, gathered from real life or from the school lessons of the day, give the teacher the opportunity to impart the great lessons of morality and to teach the duties the individual owes to God and his fellows.

Vital Educational Questions

The great need of emphasis upon this subject is seen not only in the alarming prevalence of vice and crime among the lower classes, but also in the fraud, embezzlement, and treachery practised in business transactions, and the demagogism and falsehood in political life.   This is a matter of vital importance to the public weal, and should awaken the interest and secure the co-operation of parents, citizens, and school officers to provide all necessary facilities for the training of teachers, and to see to it that none but those who are qualified for the responsible position shall be allowed to assume its duties.

VII

OTHER EDUCATIONAL WORK

ALL grades of schools and educational institutions are inseparably connected. Each is a vital organ of the same body. Hence the teacher who is engaged in any department of school work should be interested in all departments. If he is wise and in earnest he ought to be too large a man to confine himself to the one institution over which he presides. The president of a college or the preceptor of an academy or seminary can do much in various ways to encourage laborers in other fields, and to aid in promoting the common cause. Taking this view of the subject and acting on this principle, while at the head of Thetford Academy, I encouraged educational meetings in town, county, and State, to awaken an interest in the public mind in behalf of the public schools, which were in a deplorable condition. I had the honor of

Other Educational Work

leading in the organization of the State Teachers' Association in Vermont, which has held its annual meetings and been an increasing power for good in the State for more than fifty years, and is to-day one of the most efficient organizations of its kind in the nation.

At North Granville Seminary I took charge of a second-grade school for boys in the same village with my own school, and conducted normal classes of young ladies, under the Regents of the State of New York, for the better training of teachers of the public schools.

At Glenwood Seminary I accepted the position of superintendent of the public schools of Brattleboro, and held the office for two years; and later I held the same office in Lebanon, New Hampshire, for the same length of time. While at Glenwood I was editor and proprietor of the " Vermont School Journal" for four years, published for the aid and encouragement of the teachers in the public schools of the State. Educational literature was scarce in those days.

Reminiscences of School Life

At Tilden Seminary, while a member of the Legislature from the town of Lebanon, I introduced and carried through three bills in the interest of education, in the State of New Hampshire, viz., the bill requiring compulsory attendance in the public schools, the bill changing the district to the town system, and the bill establishing the State Normal School at Plymouth; and for six years I was supervisor or trustee of that institution.

During the forty years of my school life it was my constant aim to gather up the results of experience and study and publish the same for the benefit of others who might follow in my path. I first published "The Class Book of Prose and Poetry" with analytical tables, to be used as a text-book in parsing; next followed "The Teachers' Manual," devoted largely to the discipline of the school, taken in its broadest sense; "Home and School Training," showing the vital connection between the family and the school, and pointing out and urging the mutual and important duties of parents and teachers in their relations to each other and to their schools; "School Keeping: How To Do It," prepared for young teachers and dealing with methods of discipline and instruction. These books have passed through several editions, and some of them have been used as text-books in academies, seminaries, and normal schools, and all have been read by thousands of practical teachers all over the nation. Twenty-five years ago, by request of General John Eaton, then at the head of the National Bureau at Washington, D. C., I prepared a monograph on school management for publication by that Bureau. This and the "Class Book of Prose and Poetry" have had a circulation of more than one hundred thousand copies each. Dr. Harris, now at the head of the National Bureau, told me that this monograph had been in more demand than any pamphlet the Bureau had ever published. During all these years I have been constantly writing on educational subjects for the public press, and frequently lecturing before teachers' institutes and other educational bodies.

After forty years of constant strain upon

one set of nerves I began to feel the need of a change. I did not desire rest such as results from retirement from active life, but simply a change in the kind of labor which should require my mental and physical activity. Still I had no plans for securing this relief, or expectations of leaving my school in the near future. But in the summer of 1880 an earnest call came from Boston urging me to accept a position of partner in a well-known publishing company located in that city. After due consideration, I accepted the offer, and made arrangements to enter upon my new work late in the autumn.

This corporation was and is devoted entirely to educational work. It was not a school, but an educational publishing house. Hence the change did not remove me to a mere business life, but enabled me to continue in the same service in a new field. This was exactly what I desired. Our two educational journals, one weekly and the other monthly, our educational books and aids to teachers, and our Educational Bureau, brought us and has kept us in

constant touch with the schools and teachers
of the whole nation. Hence, this was not
only a new, but a more extended field of
labor and usefulness.

Educational journalism is a powerful
agency in moulding and directing public
opinion in the interest of public and private
schools of every grade. It is a guide and a
spring of inspiration to the teacher, supervisor, and superintendent of these schools,
the most reliable source of information upon
all educational subjects, and a bond of union
between all educators and educational organizations. The publishing and distributing
among teachers and school officers professional books and monographs applies an
important added force, working out the
same results, and introducing the best
methods of school discipline and instruction. The Educational Bureau which this
company established, the first and for several years the only one in New England, has
proved to be an important aid, if not an
indispensable agency, in the interest of
teachers and school officers. It has enabled
thousands of the one class to secure desir-

able positions, and the other class to provide competent teachers, adapted to the positions which they have to fill, at the least expense of time and money. In the Bureau thousands of applicants, for every grade and department of instruction, are registered, and their record and qualifications are on file for examination. Here superintendents and other school officers come to examine these records and to meet candidates, and are thus enabled to make wise selections to fill vacancies.

There was at first a strong prejudice among school officers against teachers' bureaus, but their practical helpfulness has proved of so great benefit to all parties interested that this hostility has, by degrees, worn away, until now only a few ignorant or bigoted independents refuse to patronize them. So great a change has been wrought in public sentiment on this subject that instead of a solitary agency in New England and one or two in the other States, as was the case twenty years ago, there are more than a " baker's dozen " in the city of Boston.

Other Educational Work

My active relations with the management of this corporation extended almost down to the present time, covering a period of fifteen years. For three years, since relinquishing my former labors as a partner, I have done continuous work on the editorial staff, and am still performing full service, at the age of eighty-three years.

I have thoroughly enjoyed my long life of service, under the guidance of an All-wise Providence, and if I have been able to do anything to aid and encourage the thousands of youth who have come under my instructions and influence, in their efforts to gain an education and positions of honor and usefulness in the world ; if I have aided them in character-building and right living, or have in any way done anything calculated to elevate the teachers' office, — I am amply paid for my service, and am sure that my laborious life has not been a failure. I am profoundly grateful to our Heavenly Father, whose guiding hand directs all our ways and "whose mercy endureth for ever."